Daughter of Oreveille

Book One of the Oreveille Cycle

Tricia Ballad

Faeland Press, Bloomington, Illinois, USA

Daughter of Oreveille by Tricia Ballad
© 2013 by Tricia Ballad. All rights reserved.

Published by: Faeland Press, Bloomington, Illinois

Cover Design by: Karri Klawiter, Art By Karri

Ballad, Tricia, 1976 – Daughter of Oreveille
ISBN: 978-0-615910-39-0
10 9 8 7 6 5 4 3 2 1
1. Fantasy 2. Romance
First Edition
Printed in the USA

DEDICATION

To Bill. Without him, Brianna's story and my own would be much less interesting.

CONTENTS

ACKNOWLEDGMENTS

A huge thank you to those brave souls who read and critiqued the first version of Daughter of Oreveille. Sara, Mary, Jen, Amelia, Tracy, and Yvette - your honesty and suggestions made all the difference in the world.

To Laura Matheson of Plains Text editing, I owe more than simple thanks. You saw more depth in these characters than I even realized was there. I may never write another word without passing it by you first!

Shauntelle Hamlett, you are one of those rare people who is both a dear friend and a trusted advisor. Dear reader: You are reading this book because I listened to Shauntelle's advice.

And of course, my husband Bill, without whom the sword fighting scenes would be ridiculously inaccurate.

CHAPTER ONE

May 1649. Isle of Oreveille, Faeland Sea.

Brianna walked silently through the grove of banana trees. Their wide, flat leaves offered welcome relief from the afternoon sun. She absent-mindedly fingered the moonstone that swayed from a delicate golden chain at her throat. Communing with her chosen elements of Earth and Air helped tune out the incessant droning of her companion.

"It really is a beautiful estate, Mademoiselle Oreveille. But surely you can see how neglected it will become once your father retires. An island such as yours requires constant care," Alston clearly mistook her silence for agreement.

"Stepfather," Brianna murmured, coming out of her trance before she gave into the temptation to float away like one of the thousands of fuchsia blossoms that had drifted down from the trees to litter the ground beneath her feet.

"A little hot to be out walking," A lighter male voice filtered through her consciousness, still clouded from her too-short time within the elements. She opened her eyes and saw Gabriel pruning the trees. His deep black eyes contrasted sharply with his sandy brown hair and weathered skin. Those eyes never let her forget that he was of Fae blood, despite his human mother. Brianna smiled, remembering the many long, happy childhood hours she and Gabriel spent climbing these old trees, and she envied him now as he sat amongst the limbs while she was forced to walk the lane with this arrogant son of a...

"You dare speak so to the Daughter of Oreveille?" Alston Feurlet sneered. "Get back to work, before the overseer has you flogged!" He raised his head taller and walked down the path. "Brianna, this is exactly what I was telling you about. Even the servants have begun to disrespect the authority of your House!"

Brianna glanced at Gabriel and rolled her eyes in disgust at Alston's back. Gabriel grinned and bowed in mocking subservience. Brianna stopped on the path and spoke.

"There may be truth in what you say, Monsieur Feurlet. But fear not, I would not dream of burdening a man such as yourself with such a large estate."

Alston stopped and turned to face Brianna, ready to protest her misunderstanding. She held up her hand to silence him, a gesture usually reserved for servants and human slaves. Brianna was careful not to smile at the look of shock on his aristocratic face.

"I would sooner marry Gabriel than you. He, at least, understands how to care for the trees." Finally, she allowed herself to smile.

Alston's back stiffened at the insult, however sweetly delivered. He turned and bowed to Brianna. "Forgive me for overstepping my bounds, Mademoiselle Oreveille. I shan't waste any more of your time. Perhaps we shall meet again as friends."

"Perhaps," she replied. Brianna stood still, her face carefully neutral, until Alston passed through the orchard toward the dock.

When he was finally out of earshot, she shuddered. "Horrid man!" She spat out the words and leaned against the banana tree where her oldest friend still perched. "What do you think, Gabriel? Is the island so unruly, simply because I have not yet married? I know my mother's husband does not care for the property as well as he should. But I cannot think that replacing him with a man such as that," she gestured toward the departing Alston Feurlet, "would be an improvement."

Gabriel dropped his shears as he swung down from the branch, landing lightly on his feet. He stood next to Brianna, although she noticed sadly that he did not stand as comfortably or as near to her as he once did.

"Me and Da, we keep things running as best we can. We need to post nightly guards, and regular patrols, but without direct orders from the Master of the House, they don't listen to me," he gestured toward the slave village.

Brianna smiled. "Are you looking to move up in the world? Perhaps I could convince my mother's husband to name you steward. Then they would listen to you," she offered, reaching across the space between them to take his hand. Her smile faded when his arm stiffened at her touch.

"Leave me to the trees," Gabriel mumbled. "If I don't get them pruned by sunset, I'll get that flogging your Monsieur Feurlet was so keen on! If the Master's in the mood to listen, ask him to order patrols."

Brianna sighed. "If you like." She hesitated, wishing she could recapture the easy camaraderie of the banana grove.

Gabriel nodded as he picked up his tools and moved on to the next tree in the row without looking back.

Brianna watched him study the branches for a moment, then resolutely made her way back to the main house to explain to her mother why she had rejected yet another fine young man from an old and powerful family.

CHAPTER TWO

Gabriel held his breath as he stared up at the branches of the banana tree, listening for Brianna's footsteps. As she walked away, he turned and allowed himself a glimpse of the woman he loved. Her obsidian hair was pinned in an impossibly complicated arrangement, with a single ringlet allowed to escape to adorn her right shoulder. The glossy black curl contrasted with the pearlescent skin she had favored since they were children.

"You cursed fool…" he muttered to himself, looking down at his own drab, tanned arms. His father may be a Fae, but Gabriel had not inherited the ability to alter his appearance any more than he could use other forms of power. Brianna's face, lit by the glowing symbol of her House above her eyes, remained in his mind. That mark glowed brighter than ever when she took his hand, reminding him not to forget who she was. And who he was not.

Gabriel straightened his shoulders and began the walk down to the slave village. Brianna might tie his heart in knots, but dwelling on it would not do anyone any good. It was well past time he took the boys to patrol the island, and the long walk around the perimeter would clear his mind. Oreveille was situated at the nexus of two borders, yet its strategic importance was easily overlooked if all you saw was the beauty of the place. The island stood where the outer depths of the Caribbean gathered into the massive, ancient volcanic crater that held the Faeland Sea.

The House of Oreveille had been established five thousand years ago to guard this part of the Faeland from the constant threat of kraken and leviathan, as well as bands of jotnar brave – or stupid – enough to sail the rough waters of the Atlantic in their raiding.

"And the Fae are an easy target," Gabriel said to himself. "They may have power, but not many of them can wield a sword like he means it."

He reached the small two-room cottage he shared with his father, the island's overseer. It wasn't large, but the glass windows were intact and his father had even built a front porch, giving himself and his son a place to sit in the evenings to avoid the stifling heat indoors. Once, years ago, it had been painted a cheerful yellow and white, and while the paint was faded now and peeling in places, it was still in better repair than most of the cottages in the village.

Several such cottages were built in a ring around the slave cabins. The outdoor servants, those with half-Fae blood, were allowed to live in them, and were expected to keep order and deal with any problems with the human slaves. The dirt paths between the haphazardly placed slave cabins alternated between dust and mud, depending on the season. The wretched beings who lived in them were usually captives, poor fools who wandered too close to the border between Gaia and the Faeland. Some few, such as himself, had been born here, but most were not.

There were perhaps a dozen half-Fae and human men in the village when he approached. The half-Fae stood idly, watching the human men rebuild one of the sewage ditches that ran through the place. After too many heavy storms, the ditches often collapsed, and had to be re-dug.

"Shore it up with timbers this time, boys!" Gabriel shouted.

One of the half-Fae turned to face him. William. When they were children, he had boasted of his plans to replace Gabriel's father as overseer. "Waste of good wood. We've got plenty of humans to dig out the ditches when they collapse."

"Aye, but the smell until they get it dug out is something terrible," Gabriel countered. He watched the shirtless human men digging knee-deep in filth and mud. "Fix it properly this time and we won't have to do this every three months."

The other man grunted and turned back to the work at hand. "Keep digging!" he commanded, catching sight of a human who had straightened up to get a breath of fresh air.

Gabriel grimaced at the sound of the whip cracking through the air. "It's well past time to patrol the borders, boys. I need a half dozen men."

"What do you need so many men for?" William sneered. "Afraid you might meet up with a stray dog and need reinforcements?"

Gabriel did not answer. He had learned long ago that the only way to win an argument was with silence.

"These men are needed here. This ditch must be dug out before nightfall." William was going to be stubborn.

"Really? You need so many just to watch a handful of humans? Afraid they might turn on you?" Gabriel answered.

"They must be properly supervised. We've had three escape attempts this month!"

Gabriel nodded. He had turned a blind eye to all three of them, and the last two had made it to open waters. He looked at the wretched man whose crime had been stealing a breath of fresh air. Two lines of crimson decorated his bare back. Perhaps there would be a fourth escape attempt this month, Gabriel mused.

"Fine. Then I'll patrol alone. So that you will have nothing more to fear than your own filth," Gabriel replied, walking away.

This was not the first time he had walked the border of the island alone. Truth be told, he preferred it this way.

The human slaves cringed away from him and kept huddled in pairs and small groups, and the other half-Fae tried to imitate their full-blooded masters in arrogance. Gabriel shrugged. He needed to pay attention to the sea anyhow, not his companions.

Gabriel walked for the better part of an hour before he saw tracks in the wet sand. They were small, like the footprints of a newborn child.

"Gobeleins," Gabriel swore. They were often used as scouts by larger and more intelligent creatures.

He knelt down to examine the tracks. They were headed inward toward the stables. The Oreveille warhorses were bred to carry a man in full armor. A gobelein would not be able to reach its halter, let alone try to steal one. They were probably simply there to gather information. He had to be sure the gobelein scout did not return to his masters. They were not particularly intelligent, but were intensely loyal to the jotnar that fed them and kept their dens safe from predators. Where there were gobelein scouts, there were raiders nearby.

"Shouldn't have wasted time arguing," he muttered to himself as he broke into a run. Perhaps if he could capture the gobeleins, the Master of the House would take his insistence upon a night watch seriously. He could not hope to patrol the entire island himself.

Gabriel heard the horses kicking and neighing before he reached the stables. Something had them agitated. He slowed to a walk and listened as he entered the practice yard. The stable had stalls for close to fifty horses, although it was mostly empty these days. If he paid attention the horses would save him the trouble of searching every stall. He slipped inside and blinked, giving his eyes time to adjust to the dim light.

The sound of splintering wood and the high-pitched shriek of the gobelein drowned out the sounds of nervous horses.

He reached the agitated horse and found the gobelein standing outside the stall. It looked like a hideously oversized infant, about two feet tall and naked except for a thin layer of coarse hair covering its body. There was no innocence in this creature, however, which made its appearance all the more disturbing. The legend was that these creatures were half-Fae children left on beaches and hillsides to die, to save their Fae mothers the embarrassment of acknowledging a tryst with a human man. According to the stories, jotnar would find them, and the ones that weren't eaten on the spot were brought back to the creatures' dens and raised as their own. Gobeleins were the result.

"It would explain their loyalty," Gabriel mused as he drew his sword and pulled his knife from his belt. Unlike the Fae and even most half-Fae, Gabriel had no ability to wield power, so he learned to rely on his fists, and later, his sword. Fae power wasn't everything.

The gobelein looked up and shrieked again. In the back of the stable, Gabriel heard scuffling footsteps. The second gobelein had fled. He would chase it down, but first he would have to deal with this one.

As the stable door slammed shut, the terrified gobelein pulled a filthy knife from its pouch and charged.

Gabriel held his sword low and easily parried the gobelein's clumsy swipe at his knees. In an instant, he brought his own knife up, gutting the creature.

He stepped over the mess and ran out the back door, following the tracks toward the docks. He had to catch the beast before it made it offshore, or there would surely be another jotnar raid. They lost more men and horses in every raid, and every time, the huge beasts made it closer and closer to the main house. Gabriel was not certain how many more times the meager defenses of Oreveille would withstand them.

With every step, his stomach clenched harder. The docks were in sight, but the gobelein was gone. He was too late. Gabriel stopped at the water's edge, scanning for a boat, but the horizon was clear. There was nothing more he could do but go back and clean up the mess in the stable.

Half an hour later, he wrapped the dead gobelein in a length of rough burlap and carried it to the Great House. Perhaps, if he dumped the bloody evidence at his feet, the Master of the house would listen to him and order a night watch.

From the front, the Great House was perfect and terrifying. Its white marble columns seemed to stretch into the clouds, and every one of the dozens of windows seemed like an eye, staring at any poor soul who had to walk that path to the grand entrance. Gabriel and the other servants were lucky enough to be spared this fate. They approached the Great House from the rear, where it was less meticulously maintained, and therefore less intimidating.

Gabriel shifted his burden onto one shoulder as he veered away from the front of the house. As he approached the rear entrance, Madame Oreveille's glamour began to fade, and the bare, weathered wood showed through. Gabriel could not remember when the men had last been called to work on the Great House, but his father told stories of being a child and carrying water and buckets of nails for the men who kept the ancient building alive. He touched the brittle wood as he rounded the corner to the back of the house. It needed to be repaired, almost as badly as some of the cabins in the slave village, but the Master of the house wasn't likely to bother as long as the Mistress could keep the appearance of grandeur at the front.

As he walked in the servant's door, past the kitchen, the cook called out to him. "Gabriel, me boy - come say hello to an old woman!"

Gabriel shook his head. "Got a package to deliver to His Drunkenness. If he doesn't toss me out of the house, I'll stop and drink a cup of tea with you."

"Get on with you then," she replied. Gabriel smiled at the fondness in her voice. After his mother disappeared all those years ago, she had taken him in and loved him like one of her own.

He trudged up the narrow, dark staircase at the rear of the house. The center of each stair was worn to a softness that cupped the servants' tired feet. A small comfort in a house designed more for show than warmth and happiness.

At last, Gabriel reached the fifth floor and entered the main part of the house. The Master of the house spent a few hours in his study overlooking the lake and the stables, before making his way to the billiard room below. He shifted the hastily wrapped body to his other shoulder and knocked.

A snore was the only reply he got.

Gabriel knocked again, louder this time, and again heard only snoring from within. He tried the doorknob. It was locked, as he suspected. Gabriel swore under his breath, and aimed a single kick at the rotting wood in the center of the door. It splintered, and the snoring abruptly stopped. Gabriel cleared away enough fragments of the door to reach through and unlock it.

"What the Devil did you do to my door?" the man inside spluttered.

"It needed fixed anyway," Gabriel replied. "Sir," he added after a long moment of silence.

"Get out of my study!" the Master of the house screeched, pointing at what was left of his door.

Gabriel dumped the dead gobelein on the dusty mahogany desk covered with half-filled ledgers and unopened letters. "Trouble's on its way."

The other man simply stared. In the ballroom, glamour gave him the look of a man at his prime. Here, in his study, Gabriel saw him as he was - his yellowed skin sallow and hanging, his hair, once glistening black, now thin and dulled with streaks of grey. He reached a bony hand instinctively toward the crystal decanter of brandy - the only thing in the room that saw frequent use.

"Master of Oreveille," Gabriel spoke with military formality, hoping to jar the man's memories of former glories. "I captured this gobelein scout in the stables. Its companion escaped before I could catch it, and is at this moment reporting back to its masters. Your orders, sir?"

"Orders?" The master of the house of Oreveille slung back a snifter of brandy. "Two gobeleins hardly seems like a threat," he slurred. "Get back to your work. And fix my door!" his voice rose as he refilled his glass.

Gabriel turned and left. As he walked down to the kitchen for a cup of tea he grinned, wondering how long it would take the Master to realize he had left the dead gobelein behind.

CHAPTER THREE

Madame Riet was late. Brianna wandered through the shaded garden, skipping a nut across the still afternoon air. She was beginning to hope her teacher had forgotten their lesson. There were only so many times a girl could float the same tiny stone before she went mad! Besides, Brianna had other things on her mind. Gabriel was worried about the jotnar, but he would barely look at her when she offered him the authority to set up the watch he believed necessary. She would do what she could to convince her stepfather to order a night watch, but until she took her place as Matriarch, he was not likely to listen. And Mother simply ignored anything outside the Council chambers. Still, she had to try. Perhaps, if she could catch him tomorrow, early in the day...

Brianna groaned as she saw the unmistakable form of Madame Riet leaving the House. By the time she finished her exercises, it would be too late to avoid having another difficult conversation with her mother about suitable young men.

"Good morning, Daughter of the House," Madame Riet always began their lessons with a formal greeting. "I see you've already begun your practice," she added, seeing the nut floating and skipping across the air in front of Brianna.

Brianna inclined her head, letting the nut drop to the ground. "Good morning, Teacher."

"Pick it up. This time, instead of letting the Air current take the nut where it will, place the nut on the tip of the leaf," Madame Riet held a dogwood branch steady.

Brianna sighed. A pack of sea jotnar could be anchored just offshore, and she was trapped here balancing nuts instead of learning something useful. She glanced at the nut on the ground and reached out a wisp of her spirit to the Air surrounding it. The nut shot up toward the tree and dropped, missing the branch.

"Again. Recall, the essence of Power is control," Madame Riet reprimanded.

"Perhaps, if we did something more interesting…" Brianna thought, grateful for once that she did not have the gift of Spirit Walking. Communicating through the mists was convenient, but she enjoyed the freedom to say what she liked within her Spirit without risk of being overheard.

For the next hour, Brianna raised the same nut, each time more slowly than the last, and placed it precisely on the tip of a dogwood leaf.

"Better," Madame Riet nodded her approval as Brianna's nut finally perched on the very tip of the leaf. "Do it again," she placed the nut on the ground.

Brianna concentrated and the nut rose, imperceptibly slowly, toward the tree. She placed it back on the leaf, balanced on its tip. She held it there for a long moment.

Madame Riet nodded. "Much better. We will practice again tomorrow."

"Wait. Before you go, I have been studying the other branches of Power. I wish to begin practicing outside my chosen elements." Brianna chose her words carefully.

"Master your elements before you begin to study the other branches," Madame Riet smiled. "Have patience! There is plenty of time for you to study Spirit Walking. Perhaps next year."

"Not Spirit Walking. I want to study Life and Healing," Brianna's voice was urgent. "If the jotnar wars flare up again, we will need as many healers as we can get."

"Leave the jotnar wars to the Council and the Defenders of the Houses." Madame Riet's voice was quiet.

"Please, Madame," Brianna pressed on. "Surely you have heard the rumors. If Oreveille should falter, the Faeland would suffer greatly. Teach me enough to be useful!"

Madame Riet glanced around to a patch of dry wildflowers. "Let me show you," she motioned Brianna to kneel beside her next to the flowers.

"These flowers have very little Life left in them. In a day, they will be brown and withered. If you simply give them a taste of your Life energy, they would revive. But without water, they would soon die again. It is the same with any living thing. You can infuse a dying thing with your energy to sustain them, but unless you correct whatever caused them to fall ill or injured, they will die as soon as you remove your sustaining energy."

Brianna listened, hoping to find something she had not already read in the large Oreveille library.

As Brianna watched, Madame Riet placed her hands on the Earth at the base of one withered flower.

"I am pushing just enough of my Life energy - my spirit - into the plant to give it energy to drink," she explained, her voice just above a whisper. "Now, water the plant."

Brianna looked around the garden. There was a birdbath a few feet away. She whipped the Air currents across the still pool of water, picking up droplets to rain on the wilted flowers.

Madame Riet looked up, her mouth pursed in disapproval. "Control, Brianna, not raw Power. Keep that in mind as you try to revive the other flower."

Brianna did as she was told, placing her hands on either side of the dry stem. The Earth was warm and dry. She pushed her Spirit into the Earth to find the plant's roots. She pushed again, this time encouraging the roots to drink up her Spirit as they would the water that had long since dried up from this patch of Earth.

Brianna gasped, as she found her awareness inside the brownish-green stem of the flower. She was starving, too exhausted to reach down for the nourishing dampness below the dust. The sun burned, unceasing.

She pulled her Spirit out of the plant, and recalled her teacher's admonition to use control. Once again Brianna whipped the Air near the birdbath, but this time she spun the currents into a small cone that would carry the water to the dying plants.

Brianna shivered as the water drenched the plant's roots. She felt its cold moisture drawing up the stem, feeding her. She pushed her Spirit deeper into the plant, hoping to feel its flower open. The sun no longer burned, but she was heated from roots to the tip of her stem.

"Brianna!" Madame Riet's voice echoed faintly, but Brianna did not listen. The warmth of the healing was so pleasant!

"Brianna," This time Madame Riet came to her Spirit, through the Mists. "Leave the flower. The lesson is finished."

"But Madame..." Brianna began to argue.

"Now, Brianna."

Brianna felt her Spirit being pulled out of the intense warmth of the flower. She blinked as she opened her eyes, seeing the garden and the two healed flowers again. The first was still slightly bent and brown, but did not look as dead as it had a few moments before. The second, her flower, glowed with Power and had grown almost as tall as Brianna. She stood beside it and laughed. "I did it! I healed the little flower, and now look! It is amazing!" Her smile faded when she saw her teacher's face.

"You lost control," Madame Riet scolded. "You put too much of your Spirit into that absurd flower. If I had not pulled you out, you could have become soul-bound to a garden flower! What use would you be to anyone, if you were pulled into the Mists when this flower dies?"

"I did not realize..." Brianna began.

"Until you master the art of control, you will not risk yourself by playing with any Power beyond the Elements," Madame Riet commanded.

Brianna lowered her head, hoping her teacher would not see the tears - or the defiance - in her eyes.

CHAPTER FOUR

Brianna waited for her mother in the drawing room sipping wild strawberry tea mixed with a sprig of thyme. She would need all the courage the herbs could help her muster, to tell Madame D'Oreveille that she had dismissed Alston Feurlet.

There had been more than the usual number of slave escapes recently, and the Matriarchs of the Great Houses seemed utterly incapable of understanding the phenomenon. Brianna had tried to explain the plight of the captured humans, but Mother had not listened. Perhaps, once she married and took her place on the council, Brianna could make them listen. She would stop the practice of raiding Gaia and luring the unsuspecting creatures to the Faeland.

Brianna took another sip of her tea. She would deal with the human problem another time. Right now, she had more immediate battles to fight. If the council meeting were contentious, Madame D'Oreveille would not be in the mood to consider such petty concerns as her daughter's happiness. She picked up her tea and took a long sip of the strong, sweet brew.

"Brianna. Are you indoors already? You were to go walking with Monsieur Feurlet this afternoon."

"Yes, Mother. I went walking with him. He became quite indisposed and left rather abruptly," Brianna answered evenly.

"Did he? Monsieur Feurlet is the third young man in as many weeks who has become indisposed after walking with you. I suppose you took him down to the slave village and ranted about the creatures until he fled?" She gestured to a servant to bring her tea.

"I did not, Mother. We walked in the orchards. Honestly, I begin to wonder if there is a single young man in all the Faeland who does not whimper and flee at the thought of a brisk walk. This is a serious failing that will have repercussions throughout Fae society. Perhaps you should speak to the Ladies of the Council about their sons."

"Brianna. Enough of your sparring. What grave sin did this one commit to cause you to drive him out?"

"He was unsuitable," Brianna took another sip of her tea.

"As are they all. They are but men. You must choose one of them, before you are left with no suitors at all," her mother answered.

"And would that truly be such a tragedy?" Brianna demanded, setting down her teacup with more force than she intended. "If these young men aren't suitable for a walk around the estate, how could one of them possibly hope to administer it and care for it, let alone provide companionship and respite when I take my place on the Council?"

Madame D'Oreveille laughed, and sat down next to her daughter. "My dear, do not look to a man for companionship!"

Brianna winced at the bitterness her mother usually kept hidden.

"They are very nice," Madame D'Oreveille continued, "and they have their place, but if you want a friend, look to the young ladies of your acquaintance. Better to deepen those friendships, for some of them will become your greatest allies when their mothers and I step down."

Brianna took a deep breath. "Yes, Mother. But ..."

"But - you do need a husband, dear," her mother interrupted. "You simply cannot manage an estate of this size, as well as your responsibilities to the council, and your social obligations. It is too much for anyone." The glamour that kept Madame D'Oreveille's appearance so faultlessly strong wavered for a moment. "Find some nice young man from a strong House, and stop worrying so much about liking him. You needn't spend any significant time at all with him once you have a daughter to ensure the survival of the House."

Brianna sighed. "Mother. If I cannot stand the sight of him, why would I entrust him to manage all I hold dear?"

"Because they all know, or they quickly learn, that no Lady of the Faeland trusts her husband with anything beyond his allowance." Madame D'Oreveille spoke clinically. "Your maids will keep you informed. You can take appropriate steps if your husband neglects his duties."

"The way your husband neglects his duties?" Brianna thought, being careful to keep the disgust she felt out of her expression. Bringing up the shabbiness of the estate would not help matters any. Better to stick to the main point.

"You make marriage sound like such a practical business." Brianna sighed. "Would it be so horrible to fall in love? It does happen, you know."

"Yes dear. It does happen. Just don't let such things cloud your judgment, and don't put off choosing a husband for very much longer. If the jotnar wars flare up again, we will be overwhelmed, and they will get past the Isle of Oreveille to the interior of the Faeland. Our House will fall."

Brianna looked up in shock. "I can take care of the jotnar, mother. Is this not what I have trained for - to defend Oreveille?"

Madame Oreveille set down her tea. "No. You have been raised to rule the Fae, not to die in some obscure battlefield. Choose a husband with good connections who will strengthen the House of Oreveille, and concentrate on your own duties. And do it soon. The Summer Solstice is in a fortnight – announce your choice at the Masquerade!"

"How do you propose that I find a suitable young man in so short a time?" Brianna objected.

"You might start by giving Monsieur Dechaund a chance when he and his Mother dine with us tomorrow evening, instead of driving him off at the first sign of imperfection." Madame D'Oreveille said pointedly. "The House of Dechaund may not be my first choice of allies, but they have amassed a significant fortune and have connections that may prove helpful in shoring up our own position."

CHAPTER FIVE

As the late afternoon sun streaked through the lace curtains, Brianna stood while her maid arranged the complicated folds of her skirt. Each tuck had to be tied to a hidden loop so as to appear artless.

Brianna recalled her mother's warning. The fate of Oreveille rested on Brianna's ability to secure the borderlands by making an alliance with a powerful House. She glared at her reflection in the full-length mirror. If her mother had not married that stupid drunkard, Brianna could have been practicing her exercises or doing something useful instead of being dressed up like a porcelain doll. Who was Madame Oreveille to instruct anyone on marriage? Brianna never understood how her mother could have chosen such a worthless man so soon after her father's death. Father would never have allowed Oreveille to become a weak point in the defense of the Faeland.

She took as deep a breath as her gown would allow. Dwelling on such things would do her no good. Right now, she simply had to concentrate on surviving an evening with Madame and Monsieur Dechaund. Perhaps, if she were lucky, he would have something original to say.

"Thank you, Clarisse," Brianna said as she left the sanctuary of her dressing room to face her mother and the family Dechaund.

She heard male laughter as the butler silently opened the parlor door. "I travel through the Faeland, come out on the other side of Gaia, acquire the spices they want so badly, go back through the Faeland, and sell the whole lot to the merchants in England, and not one of them can figure out how I can make six trips to India in a single year!"

Brianna paused in the doorway, taking in the scene. Her mother and Madame Dechaund sat together discussing the recent increase in raids on the borderlands. Her stepfather stood near the large stone fireplace with a man Brianna did not know. He was taller than Monsieur Oreveille, with silvery blond hair that covered the Mark of his House. Age was always difficult to guess with the Fae, but she saw the distinctive look of experience in his grey eyes.

"Brianna, Daughter of Oreveille," the butler announced.

Laughter and conversation fell silent at Brianna's entrance. The man crossed the room to greet her. He moved with a sense of efficient purpose that reminded Brianna of something she could not quite place.

"So. You're the famed D'Oreveille," he stated. Brianna had the uncomfortable sense that he was measuring her, much as he measured spices in Gaia. "Cordov Dechaund. Pleased to make your acquaintance," he added, raising her hand to his lips.

Brianna nodded and pulled her hand away. Perhaps it was simply the cool silver tones of his skin, but his hand seemed to chill her fingers. "Good evening Monsieur Dechaund. So glad you could join us this evening." Cordov raised an eyebrow at her, but did not reply. She took a seat between the two Matriarchs.

"You spend most of your time traveling?" Madame Oreveille asked, glancing at Brianna.

Cordov nodded. "I have a fleet of six ships anchored here in the Faeland Sea, and another four in Gaia, near the Indies. All of them captained by solid men who know better than to cross me."

"How fortunate that you were in this part of the Faeland right now. Will you be staying for the Solstice?" Madame Oreveille pressed on.

Cordov smiled at Brianna. "I'm planning to stay here in the borderlands for some time, actually."

Brianna took a glass of cordial from the delicate silver tray hovering at her elbow. It stayed perfectly still while she selected her glass, then moved on gracefully as though carried by an invisible hand.

"Have the humans lost their taste in spices, or are you investigating business ventures closer to home?" Brianna asked, eyeing Cordov over the rim of her glass.

"Laying low, actually," he replied. Brianna was surprised at his blunt tone. "The Queen and King of this cycle have only recently crossed over into the mists. There isn't much time before the pathways between the Faeland and Gaia close. I'd rather not find myself trapped on the wrong side for a generation or more until the new pair meet, and the pathways open up again."

Madame Oreveille took a sip of her cordial, glancing at Madame Dechaund. "I had not been informed that the cycles were so close to shifting."

"With the recent unpleasantness at Oreveille, I did not want to concern you. Cordov only brought word of the King and Queen's departure when he returned from Gaia a few days ago," Madame Dechaund answered.

"I see," Madame Oreveille replied lightly, despite the irritation in her eyes. She turned to Cordov. "You plan to remain in the borderlands until the new King and Queen are brought together, then return to your ventures in Gaia?"

Cordov glanced at Brianna as she toyed with her moonstone. "Perhaps. There are several possibilities in play right now."

"Dinner is served, Madame," The butler opened the door between the parlor and the dining room.

Absently, Brianna followed the others into the larger room. The head chair slid out without a sound. Madame Oreveille sat and waved a hand to the rest of the room.

Brianna's chair slid out next, followed by chairs for their guests and Monsieur Oreveille. Cordov sat at Brianna's left, but much to her relief, he did not insist upon conversation in order to enjoy his meal.

The King and Queen had departed into the mists. Something bothered Brianna about Madame Dechaund's casual mention of their deaths. The King of this cycle was a Fae nobleman of one of the lesser Houses. Brianna had known him when they were children. He was only a few years older than she was, and certainly not old enough to grow old. Even if he had taken on the human lifespan of his Queen, he should not be dead yet. And yet Cordov and Madame Dechaund did not seem disturbed. Brianna sighed. Her mother's only concern seemed to be that she had not been the first to know.

"What have you heard about the jotnar wars?" Brianna glanced at her stepfather. He set his glass of wine down and waited for Cordov's response.

Cordov's stormy eyes darkened. "You never know what the creatures will do," he answered. "But when the cycles shift, resources become scarce. They always raid more between cycles, and when the magic levels are low."

Brianna looked up. Gabriel had told her about the possibility of raids and the need for increased patrols, and she had promised to try to convince her stepfather to order the patrols. As usual, she assumed the old man had ignored her, but perhaps something of the situation had gotten through to him.

While Cordov and her parents discussed the possibilities of another flare-up in the jotnar wars,

Brianna allowed her mind to wander as the servants served course after course. Gabriel had been concerned too, when she had gone down to his cabin at the edge of the slave village the night before. She smiled. He and his father, Ardiel, had been finishing their evening meal on the porch, where the breeze cooled the air. She sat on a low, handmade bench next to Gabriel and listened to his father tell legends from Gaia. She loved the ones about Robin and the Maiden, and the great Gaian King, Arthur. Long before the stories were finished, Brianna had leaned against Gabriel, enjoying the warmth of his body against the humid chill of the night breeze. She felt more contentment on that rough bench beside Gabriel than when she pulled her spirit into her favorite moonstone.

"Do you not agree, Brianna?" Madame Oreveille's voice broke jarred her out of her daydream.

"Of course, Mother," she replied automatically. It was always easier to agree with Madame Oreveille than to admit that she had not been listening to the conversation.

"Then it is settled. Monsieur Dechaund, we look forward to your return tomorrow."

Brianna glanced at Cordov, who simply bowed his head briefly. "Until tomorrow then, D'Oreveille."

"Tomorrow," Brianna echoed as Cordov and Madame Dechaund departed.

CHAPTER SIX

Gabriel saw her first, from his vantage point in the trees. Brianna was running toward the grove, carrying a practice sword. He leapt down and called to his father and the other gardeners. "There's trouble boys!"

At his warning, half a dozen human and half-Fae men, all hardened from days of sun and labor, swung down from the trees and picked up their tools. They held hoes and hatchets like weapons, and Gabriel had seen every one of them use the tools to kill or defend themselves. Raids did not happen often, but they happened often enough to keep everyone alert.

"Jotnar," Brianna announced, as she tried to catch her breath. "At the stable."

While the other men fell in behind her, ready for battle, Gabriel ran ahead. He had been expecting this.

As he crested the hill between the grove and the stable yard, he stopped, listening to the guttural howls of the beasts and the screaming of men and horses. He could only see one jotnar in the stable yard feasting on the entrails of a stable hand. It squatted on massive haunches, rocking ecstatically as it ate. Gabriel could only guess how many others were already inside the stables.

Gabriel took in the scene and stopped Brianna before she came over the top of the hill. She had joined her mother in the defense of the Isle before, and was no stranger to blood, but this time she was alone. "Go back to the house, Bri. Get reinforcements. Let me and the boys do what we can here." He spoke quietly, his gentle voice out of place in the midst of so much carnage.

Brianna shook her head and kept going. "No. I will not run away and hide. Mother has called for every able-bodied Fae on the estate. They will be here soon. Perhaps we can save the horses at least." She drew her sword. "Let's go, boys."

Gabriel cursed lightly, and kept one step ahead of her. As they walked slowly down the short hill, the stench of fresh, hot blood and matted jotnar fur was nauseating.

Brianna stopped short and threw out her hands as a gust of wind cut through the smell. The jotnar looked up from its kill just long enough to see the group of Fae coming towards it. As it choked on the dust kicked up by the wind, Gabriel nodded to the other men. They knew what to do, and fanned out to flank the creature. He stayed close to Brianna. Normally, Madame Oreveille would stun the beast and hold it immobile long enough for Gabriel and the other men to butcher it, but Brianna seemed to have other ideas.

"Die."

Gabriel heard the whispered command, although he doubted the jotnar did. He looked at the young Fae woman, and realized just how much power she could command. The Mark on her forehead glowed, almost blinding him to the madness in her eyes.

The wind blew harder, nearly knocking Gabriel to the ground. It swirled around the jotnar and what was left of the stable hand, lifting them off the ground.

"Higher!" Brianna shrieked.

"Brianna," Gabriel wondered if she would hear him, as furious as she was. "Don't push yourself. There may be more inside."

The wind carried the jotnar higher and higher, until the beast rose toward the clouds.

"Brianna!" Gabriel could see the sweat beading on the girl's temples. She was going to exhaust herself before the battle was even begun.

Brianna took a deep, shuddering breath. "Enough." Her eyes cleared as she watched the jotnar fall to the ground. As soon as it landed, she ran toward the stable.

Gabriel followed, ready for the next wave of the attack, even if Brianna was not.

CHAPTER SEVEN

Brianna retched at the sight of the half-eaten man in the center of the yard. She threw her hands out and a gust of wind caught the loose dust in front of the beast, clogging its lungs just enough to capture its attention.

Brianna stared deeply into its uncomprehending eyes.

"Die," she whispered as the mark of Oreveille across her forehead glowed brighter. She concentrated, releasing her spirit into the loose dirt of the yard and the soft breeze that always blew off the water.

Once again, the dust began to churn. The breeze intensified as Brianna summoned the wild winds of the Faeland Sea. The dirt rose, formed into a perfectly inverted cone by the circling winds. Higher and higher Brianna's spirit danced on the Air as it whipped around the loose Earth until it lifted the 800-pound jotnar like a dead leaf.

"Higher!" Brianna shrieked, her eyes locked on the terrified beast.

The wind obeyed, and she whirled faster and higher until she could no longer hear the jotnar's screams over the roar of the tornado.

"Enough," she commanded as she pulled her spirit out of the Air and back into her body. The wind ceased as suddenly as it had begun, and without the Air to hold it up, the cone of Earth collapsed. The jotnar flailed helplessly as it fell over a thousand feet to the solid ground of the stable yard.

Brianna's face dripped with sweat.

"Get rid of that," Gabriel ordered the men, nodding at the stunned jotnar. Several of the gardeners broke away from the group and systematically butchered the creature.

Brianna made her way past the stable yard into the barn.

"Wait!" Gabriel called, but Brianna did not stop.

"We must save the horses!" She called as she strode into the darkness of the stable.

Just inside, another jotnar fought to control Cragg. Once, the stallion had been her father's favorite warhorse. Since his death, Cragg had been half-wild. No man or Fae had been able to mount him, and most had given up trying. Brianna smiled. The giant horse did not follow the jotnar willingly.

Two more stable hands lie crumpled on the floor.

"Begone!" Brianna commanded, raising her arms to call the wind once again. Inside the stable, she could not create another tornado, but the hot gust of air was enough to slam the jotnar against the wall of the stable.

The sudden impact distracted the jotnar for a split second – just enough for it to loosen its grip on the half-wild horse. The stallion sensed its opportunity and reared up, kicking the jotnar in the face. The jotnar staggered back, unaware for several long moments that its injuries were fatal. The horse's hoof was strong enough to shatter even the thick skull of the jotnar, and drove shards of bone deep into its brain. The stallion bolted wildly out into the yard, unsure whether to rejoice in its freedom or panic at the screaming of the other horses.

Gabriel caught Brianna's arm as they walked into the dark stable. "Be careful." His voice was no longer gentle.

Brianna smiled at him in triumph. "There is nothing to worry about. The beasts do not stand a chance when I dance on the wind." She pulled her sword from its sheath and blew along the blade. Where her breath touched the steel, the Mark of Oreveille appeared.

"See? Now even if I do have to resort to my sword, it carries my spirit in the Earth of its blade." She turned away from Gabriel and ran down the narrow walkway between the stalls. "Hurry! There are more jotnar in the tack room!"

CHAPTER EIGHT

Gabriel followed Brianna into the stable. As long as the jotnar remained stunned, the others could handle it. She may be the D'Oreveille, but he was not going to let that get her killed.

Inside, he watched as she threw another gust of wind at the already struggling jotnar, throwing it against the wall. Two more bodies lay in the corner. He could not tell if the horse or the jotnar had killed them, and at the moment he did not care. They had been good men and had not stood a chance against a full-grown jotnar in close quarters. If patrols had been posted the beasts would not have gotten this far from the docks, Gabriel fumed.

He barely had time to step out of the way as the freed horse bolted out into the yard.

Brianna ran past the second jotnar without a second glance.

"Watch out!" Gabriel yelled, too late.

He saw the hairy fist of a third creature fly out of a stall just as Brianna's head passed by. He doubted she even saw what hit her as her body crumbled to the floor. He shouted over his shoulder for help as he ran to pull her limp body out of the way.

The Mark of Oreveille still glowed on the blade of Brianna's sword. Gabriel took it from her fist and advanced on the jotnar. Three good men dead and Brianna…he would not let himself think of her bloody, lifeless face. Right now, he needed to hit something. The jotnar lumbered out of the stable, it's muzzle dripping with blood.

Gabriel stepped forward, circling the beast. He swung the blade and was surprised at its lightness. The jotnar lumbered toward him, pressing him back down the walkway toward Brianna's still body. If she were dead… Again and again he swiped, slicing the beast's tough hide. He knew he was going to lose her. She despised them, but the Fae noblemen kept coming. She couldn't insult and refuse them forever. He lunged at the beast as it turned its back, and grinned at the easy wounding. She was going to have to marry one of the fools, and that would be the end of their friendship. He ducked as the jotnar swung a weighty fist at his head, and laughed. He could not call what they had a friendship any more than he could call this jotnar a swan. A man did not, even at his most closely guarded moments, think of a friend the way Gabriel dreamed of Brianna. He swung the sword - her sword - at the jotnar's face. As he circled around the confused jotnar, he saw his opening and lunged, driving the length of the blade into the base of the creature's skull.

As he yanked the sword out of the jotnar's bloody flesh, two more of the creatures stood watching. Gabriel wiped the gore from the blade, revealing the glowing Mark of Oreveille. The jotnar hesitated, then turned, and lumbered out of the back of the stable. Gabriel turned as well, and knelt beside Brianna's motionless body. If she were dead…he did not want to consider it.

The Mark of Oreveille was faded, but it was not completely gone. Gabriel let out a deep breath. She was not dead, or the Mark would have disappeared. In exhaustion and relief, he touched the intertwined lines of gold that reassured him that she lived. She was unconscious, knocked out by the force of the blow, and unaware of the chaos around her. Gabriel slowly lowered his lips to hers. She was alive, if only barely. Everything else could wait.

Tricia Ballad

CHAPTER NINE

When Brianna awoke, she floated in the warm softness of her own bed. The room was dark and quiet, although she could hear the breathing of someone sitting in the large chair beside her bed. Someone else moved quietly through the room. Slowly, Brianna opened her eyes, ready for the blinding light and intense pain she had felt in the stable. She felt a dull throbbing at the base of her skull, and her vision was unfocused and blurry, but the intensity of the pain was gone. She wondered how long she had slept and how she had gotten to her bedroom upstairs. She noticed she was no longer wearing her blood-spattered breeches and blouse. Someone had helped her change into a soft cotton nightgown.

Brianna opened her eyes wide. Surely Gabriel had not...

"How are you feeling, dear?" Her mother asked, interrupting her thoughts. "Any better?"

Brianna looked at the older woman sitting next to the bed. "A bit, I think. The pain is different."

"Yes, we've been giving you devil's claw. Can you try to sit up?" Her mother helped her to a sitting position, then handed her a teacup. "Drink. It will help with the pain."

Brianna drank the lukewarm tea and grimaced.

"Drink," her mother commanded gently.

Brianna downed the rest of the liquid in a gulp and handed the cup back to her mother. "That was horrible. I always forget how devil's claw tea tastes."

Madame D'Oreveille smiled. "Perhaps you should stop playing with jotnar then."

Brianna shuddered as memories of the fight flooded back. "I wasn't playing. That was vile, even for jotnar."

"Don't dwell on it, dear. It's over now. The men made an example of the beasts, although I do not know how effective an example it will be. These jotnar raids have become more and more frequent."

Brianna closed her eyes, remembering how her men had fought. How Gabriel stood over her and killed the jotnar who thought she was already dead. How Gabriel kissed her. Her eyes flew open. That could not be. Gabriel was her friend, and he risked his life to save hers, but surely he did not think of her so tenderly! Brianna shook her head. She must be mistaken. She must simply be confused from the blow to the head, and mixing reality and dreams.

"Brianna. Are you listening to me?"

"How did I get back to the house?" She asked.

"One of the men carried you home. He insisted on bringing you directly upstairs." Madame D'Oreveille handed Brianna's empty teacup to a waiting maid.

"Who?" Brianna pressed.

"I have no idea! One of the gardeners, perhaps," her mother replied in exasperation. "It does not matter. What is important is that you will recover, and that you will do your duty to ensure the continuity of the House of Oreveille. Do you understand?"

"Yes, Mother," Brianna replied, as she began to comprehend the older woman's warning. She shuddered at the thought of her House falling. She had seen it before. Her own maid had once been the Daughter of a noble House, before it had fallen and its people scattered.

"What can I do to repel a jotnar attack? I tried, but there were too many of them. I am not yet ready."

"Not every problem can be solved through magic and swordplay, my dear. I have spoken to Madame Dechaund about forming an alliance between our two Houses."

An alliance... Brianna recalled her mother's instruction to give Monsieur Dechaund a chance when he and his mother dined with them, and understood what she meant. Reality was more bitter than devil's claw.

"Perhaps I should rest, if we are to entertain guests tomorrow evening."

Simply shifting positions made her head spin. She carefully lay back on the mountain of pillows behind her, and closed her eyes, searching for answers. She could not allow the House of Oreveille to fall, but the thought of a marriage to a man she could scarcely tolerate was no better. She had not met Cordov personally, but she had entertained enough young men from good families to know that she wanted as little to do with them as possible.

"I will leave you to your rest, dear." Her mother's voice filtered through her tangled thoughts, and Brianna slept, dreaming of banana blossoms and warm lips that left her no question as to their intent.

CHAPTER TEN

As the late afternoon sun streaked through the lace curtains, Brianna's maid carefully helped her dress. The green velvet gown was simple and comfortable. Certainly nothing she would wear to appear in public, but it also did not require a corset. Given the sheer number of times consciousness had eluded her in the last day, Brianna was not willing to risk fainting as well. She leaned heavily on the other girl as she made her way downstairs to the drawing room.

"Thank you, Clarisse," she said as the maid arranged pillows to make Brianna as comfortable as possible.

"Anything else, m'lady?" the maid asked.

"Yes. Please summon Gabriel. I'd like to ask him about the outcome of the jotnar raid." Brianna took care to keep her voice calm and businesslike.

The maid hesitated.

"Is something wrong?" Brianna asked.

"No m'lady. It's just that … Gabriel's a gardener, Mademoiselle. Madame Oreveille might not approve of a gardener in the drawing room," Clarisse explained.

"I understand. However, I believe my mother would prefer the drawing room to my chamber above stairs. I will speak to Gabriel, and have come downstairs out of deference to my mother's sense of propriety. The drawing room will simply have to do, unless she would have me walk all the way down to the orchards," Brianna smiled.

Clarisse hid her smile as she nodded her head in assent. "I will go fetch him, Mademoiselle."

"Thank you," Brianna nodded dismissal.

Brianna sipped chamomile tea to calm her nerves while she waited. If this afternoon's conversation went the way she hoped, her mother would have to get used to Gabriel in more than just the drawing room.

Clarisse returned several moments later, with Gabriel close behind. "Mademoiselle - you wished to speak to Gabriel?"

Brianna forced her eyes to refocus as she looked up. The maid stood in the doorway, her small frame silhouetted against Gabriel's chest and shoulders. Years of outdoor work had layered muscle upon bone to sculpt a man strong enough to stand before any threat. She smiled at the poor comparison between Gabriel - whom she did not quite dare to think of as hers – and the slight frames of the Fae men she had endured for years.

"Yes, thank you," Brianna answered, setting down her teacup. Clarisse hesitated for a moment. "I will call when I am ready to go back upstairs," Brianna gently dismissed her.

"Yes, Mademoiselle," Clarisse answered, as she silently disappeared down the long hallway toward the kitchen.

Brianna looked at the man who butchered several jotnar a few days before, and whose whispered kiss was the clearest memory she took from the battle. He stood stiffly in the doorway to the drawing room, looking over Brianna's shoulder at a particularly gilded painting. Perhaps she should have tried to walk down to the orchards or the stables, she thought, regretting his discomfort.

"Gabriel... please, come sit down. I wanted to speak to you about the jotnar raid," she said, hoping to put him at ease.

Gabriel came into the room, and sat in the nearest chair he could, set across a complicated woven rug from Brianna. He continued to look beyond her, as though he were unable or unwilling to meet her eye.

Brianna frowned slightly. It was not like him to be so silent! She could usually get a story from him simply by pausing on the path. "What happened in the stable, after I was knocked out?" she pressed.

"We killed four more jotnar in the stable, including the one that cracked you, and two more outside. There were eight total, all of them dead now," Gabriel reported.

"And our men?" Brianna asked.

"Except for the stable hand, we had a few injuries, nothing life threatening. Yours was probably the worst."

"You fought like a man possessed," Brianna said quietly as she reached for her tea.

Gabriel coughed. "We all did. You can't go easy with jotnar."

"Yes," She conceded. "But you saved my life, and then carried me home," she pressed, daring him to deny it.

"Aye," he admitted.

"And…I believe…" she hesitated, searching for just the right words. She needed the truth of that kiss, but she couldn't bear the humiliation of hearing him deny it.

"And I owe you an apology," he finished for her. "I crossed one of those lines folks put there for a reason." For the first time since entering the room, he looked directly at her. Brianna saw the desperation in his eyes. "I am truly sorry, Brianna. I shouldn't have touched you, but it's done now. I'll be leaving in the morning."

"So I wasn't dreaming?" Brianna stood and hesitated for a moment before she crossed the ornate tapestry rug that separated them. She brought his rough, hardened hand to her face as though it were the most precious thing in this room full of treasures.

Gabriel looked up at her. "No, you weren't dreaming. You were lying there so still, and I didn't know if you'd live out the day. I had to kiss you once for all those times I'd been dying to speak and knew better," he confessed.

She smiled. "Gabriel. I …" her eyes closed and she swayed.

"You need to sit down," Gabriel began to stand.

"Yes," Brianna agreed. "Come, sit with me?" She asked him, not releasing his hand.

Gabriel nodded and wrapped a strong arm around her back as he guided her to the settee near the window. He joined her, although with far too much distance between them for her taste.

"The House of Oreveille is in danger," she changed the subject.

Gabriel nodded. Brianna frowned at the look of relief that passed over his face. "The jotnar are raiding more and more. I patrol as often as I can, but without regular guards all we can do is clean up the mess once they land."

"Perhaps, once I marry and my mother steps down as Matriarch, there will be a true Defender of the House of Oreveille," Brianna said, careful to keep her voice neutral.

"That would be a good day. This island hasn't been properly defended since your Da was killed in the last jotnar war," Gabriel agreed.

Brianna smiled. "I intend to choose a man very much like him. Someone who understands Oreveille and its importance," she slid closer to Gabriel, until she could feel the warmth of his thigh through the velvet of her gown. "Someone I trust. Someone... " her voice faltered and she looked for reassurance in his eyes. " Someone I love."

"You deserve such a man," Gabriel reached for her with his free hand, for she still had not let go of the other. Brushing a stray wisp of hair from her eyes, he caressed her aristocratic cheekbones, her smiling lips.

Brianna could see the battle waging between propriety and desire, and she wrapped her arms around his neck, sliding easily into his lap as she kissed him, leaving no doubt as to her intentions.

"How could I say no to you?" He asked, breathless.

"You can't," she said, twirling his hair around her finger. "So why even try?" She smiled.

Gabriel laughed, but just as quickly, his laughter died. "Brianna. You know we can't do this," he said as he gently lifted her off his lap. "You have your duty to your House, and..."

"I know my duty," Brianna snapped. "Mother made it quite clear. My duty is to replace her worthless husband with a man who can defend Oreveille from these raids and prevent another jotnar war." She looked deep into Gabriel's eyes, willing him to understand. She wished she had any ability at all in the realm of Influence, but that area of power had always eluded her. "I have yet to meet any man who can do that half as well as you."

She wound her fingers through his. "Besides, I have loved you since we were children, and would be perfectly miserable without you. Why shouldn't I do my duty and be happy at the same time?"

"No one forbid you from enjoying yourself, so long as you do your duty." came a voice from the doorway. Brianna quickly stood, and her knees would have given out from the sudden movement if Gabriel had not stood to steady her.

"Hello Mother," Brianna greeted the older woman with as much composure as she could muster. "As you see,

I have done as you asked and chosen a husband. I shall announce him at the Solstice ball."

"And have you considered the implications of your choice? This is but a powerless half-Fae, with a human mother. He will be dead within the century, leaving you in your prime," Madame Oreveille pointed out.

"Then we will enjoy the time we have," Brianna replied, not bothering to soften the defiance in her voice. "Besides, I have mastered my chosen elements, and have already begun the study of Life and Death. Perhaps…"

"No," Gabriel interrupted her. "Brianna, don't go trying to change nature. It is what it is, and we're made to die for a reason. Who knows but I'll come back as a blue jay who chatters outside your window before sunrise every morning, for the sheer joy of waking you up."

"Very well!" Brianna laughed. "Mother, may I present Gabriel, son of Ardiel?" She spoke the formalities.

"Gabriel," Madame Oreveille intoned, inclining her head ever so slightly. "You are welcome in this house."

"Madame Oreveille," Gabriel replied. Brianna noticed a hint of challenge in his smile.

"You will, of course, join us for dinner tomorrow evening," Madame Oreveille invited with all the grace of a woman accustomed to getting her way. "So that we can all get better acquainted."

Brianna smiled and took Gabriel's arm. "Just a quiet family dinner, Mother," She insisted.

"Of course, dear. You shall have a full social calendar once you announce your engagement. A quiet family dinner is just the thing," Her mother agreed. "Now, where is the downstairs maid? I'll speak to her about setting an extra place."

As Madame Oreveille swept out of the room, Brianna turned to Gabriel, her smile brighter and more carefree than authentic. "You see? All will be well."

Gabriel simply grinned. "We'll see."

CHAPTER ELEVEN

Brianna closed her eyes and leaned back against the solid trunk of an oak tree that had been ancient when her mother was a girl. As she rested, waiting for Gabriel to return, her mother's voice invaded her thoughts.

"You know, dear, you would not be the first Fae woman to enjoy the novelty of a human male," Madame Oreveille's voice echoed noiselessly in her ears.

"Leave me alone, Mother," Brianna thought. Her lips moved as she formed the words in her mind. She was never particularly good at this style of communication.

"You certainly aren't expected to marry one of them. Keep him, enjoy him, but choose a true Fae as husband. One who will not hold you back," Madame D'Oreveille made it sound so simple.

"I am in love with Gabriel, and will choose no other. Besides, you have yet to introduce me to a Fae man who could defend Oreveille half as well as Gabriel already has."

"Do not make such a declaration in haste, child. You will come to regret it, and I will not sponsor some human's widow in society."

"I have made my choice, Mother. You must make yours. Now leave me alone!" Brianna opened her eyes, hoping to dismiss her mother's spirit. The last thing she needed was bitter words in her ears as she met Gabriel's father. She touched her moonstone, and pulled her spirit into the breeze that wafted through the garden. Within her elements, she could rest, floating freely yet grounded in the timeless stability of Earth. She rested there, until she felt the vibrations of approaching footsteps. Slowly, reluctantly, she pulled her spirit out of the elements and focused her eyes on the two men who walked up the hill toward her.

She sighed. From their strides alone, Brianna could tell this would not be a happy conversation. The older man gestured emphatically as he marched, while Gabriel's back was stiffly resolute. Apparently, she was not the only one receiving parental warnings against this marriage.

Brianna sat up straighter and affixed her brightest smile. She slid to one side of the bench, leaving just enough room for Gabriel to sit next to her.

The two men stopped abruptly at the garden wall. Brianna could not hear their conversation. She could only watch helplessly as the older man turned and walked back toward the grove, leaving Gabriel alone.

"He was not pleased," Brianna spoke softly.

"No. I got quite the earful about humans and Fae, and what goes wrong when we mix," Gabriel replied.

"What? What is this horror that must happen when a Fae woman and a half-Fae man unite?" she placed particular emphasis on the words.

"Bri…" Gabriel sat down next to her and took her hands. "You know that even with my father's blood, in the eyes of this world, I am little better than a human. Power comes from the mother, and my mother was just an ordinary human girl."

"I know the laws of power. I also know Fae men. They may have mastered the elements or spirit walking, or summoning, but not one of them is half as alive as you," She leaned toward him to rest her head on his shoulder. "I do not want a socially acceptable servant to escort me to balls and administer my estate. I want a companion. A partner. A man who loves me."

Gabriel inhaled the rich oaken scent of her obsidian hair. "Brianna. I do love you – enough that I won't cost you the life you've got coming. If we marry, they'll cast you out. You'll lose your inheritance, your position, everything."

Brianna sat up and stared at him. He held tight to her hands.

"I don't care about the Matriarchs and their opinion!" Brianna declared petulantly.

"Brianna...you've seen what happens when a house is destroyed. Without a Matriarch, Oreveille will fall, and your mother cannot hold the island together much longer," Gabriel spoke quietly.

"What are you suggesting?" she asked, her voice guarded.

"Da will show me the way to Gaia. I will be able to get through. I'll find my mother, and make a fresh start," He answered, trying to keep the bitterness out of his voice.

"The cycle is ending. The king and queen have crossed into the mists."

"All the more reason for me to go now, before the pathways disappear."

"Then I'll come with you."

"The humans do not like the Fae, Bri. You would not be welcomed." Gabriel let go of her hands and looked away. "You'll do what must be done here, and I won't be here to remind you of what cannot be."

"Then I will not look Fae. I know enough glamour to pass as human," She insisted. "But I will not lose you!"

"You may wish you had, after a few years as a human man's wife. Life there isn't easy, Bri," he said, staring into the distance. "Their world is different."

"Perhaps my abilities would be lessened, but surely I would not be completely powerless!" She laughed.

Gabriel turned to look into the depths of her eyes. "It's not just about magical power. To them, a woman is hardly more than a slave. First she belongs to her father, then to her husband. You may be able to look like a human woman, but you could never act like one."

"But you would never treat me so," Brianna argued. "And I am certain the stories have been exaggerated. They always are."

Gabriel shook his head. "Our fortunes would rest on my shoulders, and I'd find a way to provide for us, but I'd not be a nobleman there any more than I am here," Gabriel continued. "It would be a simple life that I could give you. Nothing like this." He gestured from the stone house that loomed several stories above them to the manicured walled garden and the orchards and stables beyond.

"You don't frighten me!" Brianna laughed. "I can survive quite happily in the direst poverty you can conjure up, so long as you are there to comfort me. I promise." She kissed his work-hardened knuckles. "But I swear to you, I will hate every inch of this island if it costs me the one person I actually love."

Gabriel raised a hand to the back of her neck, caressing her face as he pulled her closer. "Do not hate me," he whispered against her parted lips. "If I cannot leave you here."

She made no answer, except to deepen the kiss and cling to him harder.

Tricia Ballad

CHAPTER TWELVE

Later that evening, Brianna sat at her bedroom window watching the carriages arrive. As each of them stopped at the very center of the circular drive, a footman hurried forward to assist the ladies as they stepped down. She should have know that her mother would be able to assemble most of the Council of Matriarchs – and their sons – in the space of a few hours, and that she would conveniently ignore Brianna's request for a small family dinner. She shook her head in disgust as she watched the parade. This evening would be a humiliating debacle.

"Good Gods!" she exclaimed aloud as the next carriage vomited up its royal load. "That one can't be more than nine years old." She stopped as she saw the boy's mother emerge. Madame Averiet was well known for her mastery of Influence - and her lack of a Daughter. If Brianna allowed herself to be alone with her for five minutes, she may well come out to announce her engagement to a boy hardly out of the nursery!

She looked down at her violet silk. Mother had thought of everything to remind her of the differences between herself and Gabriel. Brianna shook her head. Irritation shifted to pure disgust as she considered her next move in the game. At the moment, Mother had her at a disadvantage.

"You look beautiful, as always, m'lady," Clarisse spoke to reassure her.

Brianna nodded her head. Regardless of her personal feelings in the matter, she was the D'Oreveille, and she had her duties to perform. Clarisse trailed after her at a discreet distance as Brianna walked to the grand staircase.

Cordov waited below, deep in discussion with Madame Fuerlet and Madame Dechaund. Brianna hoped he would be too involved in whatever deal they were negotiating to notice her arrival. He was different from the other men Mother had suggested, Brianna admitted to herself, remembering Alston. Different, perhaps, but no better.

She scanned the room. Alston Fuerlet had not accompanied his mother this evening. A small smile played on Brianna's lips as she remembered his fury after her offhanded remark that she would sooner marry Gabriel than him.

Brianna's smile disappeared as she realized Gabriel was not there either. She hurried down the winding staircase toward her mother. As she reached the ballroom, the crowd seemed to part to allow her to pass.

"Brianna, dear! There you are!" Mother's voice carried a lifetime of etiquette.

"Good evening, Mother," Brianna replied. "Where is Gabriel?" She added under her breath as her mother leaned in for a kiss.

Madame Oreveille's eyes clouded briefly, but did not answer. With an imperceptible flick of her wrist, the orchestra began to play.

"Shall we have dancing, to whet the appetite?" Madame Oreveille announced.

On cue, Cordov approached Brianna and bowed. "May I?" he asked.

Automatically, Brianna nodded. "Of course. I would be delighted." For once, she was grateful for years of training. It allowed her to maneuver through the required small talk while leaving her mind free to contemplate her next move in the game. As she waltzed with Cordov, she realized that Gabriel was not in the room. Instead, Mother had assembled a party of unmarried Fae man from powerful Houses. If Mother thought one of them could win her heart, she was mistaken. Her heart was quite secure. Brianna smiled, remembering Gabriel's lips on hers only a few hours earlier. She would dance, smile through dinner, then feign a headache and have plenty of time to sneak down to his cottage to deny whatever lies Mother had told him.

"Glad you're enjoying the dance." Cordov's voice interrupted Brianna's thoughts.

"Oh. Yes. Thank you," Brianna fell silent again, and remained so throughout the dance.

At last, dinner was announced. Brianna was seated between Cordov and Madame Oreveille. She sipped her soup, hoping the conversation would flow without any direct involvement from her. Brianna wished it were Gabriel sitting beside her instead of Cordov, but it could not be helped. Perhaps he would spend the meal discussing his business ventures with Monsieur Averiet and ignore her.

As the soup dishes were silently cleared away, Madame Oreveille stood and waited until she had the full attention of her guests.

"I am very pleased to announce an alliance," she spoke brightly. Crystal goblets floated to each guest's place. "Between the House of Oreveille and the House of Dechaund."

Brianna searched her mother's face for some clue, but Madame Oreveille simply raised her glass.

"Do not embarrass the House of Oreveille." Brianna's eyes narrowed as her mother's silent voice rang through her mind.

"To Brianna, Daughter of Oreveille, and Cordov Dechaund!" Madame Oreveille toasted her daughter.

Brianna looked at the man sitting beside her. Cordov raised his glass and emptied it without a glance. Her mother looked directly into her eyes, warning her.

"How...?" Brianna had barely begun to form the thought when she felt the force of her mother's Influence.

"Do not embarrass Oreveille."

Brianna looked down the table at the gathered Matriarchs, raising her glass as well. "Thank you. May the House of Oreveille once again stand as an impossible barrier to all those who would threaten the Faeland." She smiled and engaged in the expected chatter of a girl newly engaged, aware of her mother's watchful gaze.

As soon as the guests began to move into the drawing room, Brianna made her excuses and fled upstairs. She did not have much time to make her move. Oreveille needed a defender, and she would not allow herself to be handed off like a pawn in one of her mother's games.

Inside her chamber, Brianna opened her wardrobe and felt behind the carefully folded silk stockings for a wooden box. It held a pair of intricately woven gold rings that had been created when she was just a child. She remembered hearing the goldsmith sing as he melted and twisted the glowing hot metal. She did not understand it at the time, but she knew now that the words of love and fidelity held Power.

Tucking the box inside a hidden pocket in her skirt, she ran up the servants' stairs to the top floor. She rarely had cause to come to this part of the house, but she knew what she was looking for. Her stepfather kept an office of sorts here, where he pretended to manage the estate. Brianna's eyes widened as she came to the broken down door, and saw the disarray, and the mangled gobelein corpse within. Holding a handkerchief over her mouth and nose to block some of the smell, she stepped through the destroyed doorway. The Sword of Oreveille had to be here somewhere.

The Sword of the House was always used when a Matriarch married and her husband assumed the honorary title of Defender. This time, however, Brianna intended to make the title real. She had to find the Sword!

She searched for as long as she dared, but it was not in her stepfather's office. She could not recall seeing it in the house since her father's death. Surely he had not taken such an ancient artifact to the jotnar wars!

Brianna breathed deeply. Perhaps...perhaps Mother had not bestowed the Sword of Oreveille when she remarried. Stepping carefully over the debris, Brianna made her way toward her mother's chamber.

She stopped outside the door and carefully formed an image in her mind. Closing her eyes, she saw the massive fist of a jotnar leading her favorite horse, and watched it step on the limp body of a stable hand. Brianna smiled, hoping the image would deflect her mother if the older woman should seek out her daughter's Spirit. If her plan were to have any chance of success, she had to get the Sword and get out of the house undetected.

Inside her mother's chamber, Brianna scanned the room looking for places the Sword could be hidden. Instead, it hung in plain sight at the head of her mother's bed. Focusing again on her mental image, Brianna sent her Spirit into the cold, lifeless blade. She raised it off the wall and carefully floated it to her outstretched hands.

As soon as the pommel touched her palms, she grasped its weight and ran, careful not to let her skirts get tangled in the blade. The servants' stairs were empty, and she was able to escape the house through the tiny doorway off the washing room.

In the shadows, she took a deep breath of the cool night air. She would choose this over the stuffy drawing room any evening.

She hurried toward the slave village where Gabriel lived with his father. Their cottage was larger than the others, as befitted their station as the overseer and his son. The windows were lit like warm beacons in the shadows.

As she neared the house, her footsteps slowed. The paint had been peeling since she was a young child, but Gabriel and his father kept it in good repair. Despite its shabby appearance, Brianna had always felt at home here.

Brianna balanced the Sword of Oreveille against the wall of the house. She looked intently at its blade reflecting the moonlight against the drab wall. As she concentrated, the reflection dimmed and the outline of the Sword became indistinct as it seemed to fade into the shadows. Satisfied that it would remain hidden, she opened the door.

As she entered the small doorway, she could hear Gabriel's voice inside.

"Da – it's just the evening meal. They already know who I am. I don't need to impress them with borrowed finery," he protested. "I look a fool," he added.

Brianna pushed open the simple wooden door. She saw Gabriel standing before the hearth in fine cream breeches and a black waistcoat. He looked like a man who could command the finest house in the Faeland. Brianna smiled. What a stir they would make! If she could only make him smile, he could surely charm the entire room as certainly as he had charmed her.

Except that he was not smiling tonight. The look of utter disgust on his face made her doubt herself. Perhaps Mother had been right. Gabriel would loathe the dinner parties and balls that were such a vital tool in a Matriarch's life. He turned as she hesitated in the doorway.

"Brianna," The relief in his voice washed over her. "Would you please explain to Da that I don't need to look like a man going to his own funeral just to eat dinner with your mother and stepfather?" he appealed for mercy.

Brianna walked up to him and smoothed the shoulders of his coat and straightened his tie. "Actually, you look quite debonair. I think I will actually enjoy the consternation on the Matriarchs' faces when they find out tonight that the rumors are true – that I've scorned every one of their sons in favor of a man of substance, charm, and wit." She smiled up at him, wrapping her arms around his neck. She raised her lips to offer a kiss that would silence every doubt.

He pulled her close and leaned down to claim what she offered, when his father coughed rather pointedly.

"That's about enough of that in my front room," he ordered. "I don't care who you are, you'll behave yourself in my house," the old man scolded.

Gabriel slowly straightened and released his intended bride. She took a dutiful step away, but her eyes assured

Gabriel that she fully intended to continue their discussion at a more opportune time.

"The Matriarchs are here?" Gabriel asked, finally.

"Yes. Mother invited them," Brianna replied, not bothering to hide her annoyance. "And their sons," she added.

"So much for a quiet family dinner," Gabriel said.

"She lied to us both. I did not know what she was planning until I saw the carriages arrive." Brianna turned to him. "I suppose I should have known she would do something to disrupt things. Tonight, at dinner, she announced my engagement to Cordov Dechaund."

"Dechaund," Gabriel repeated. "He's the man you're going to marry?" His voice was distant, guarded.

"Certainly not. The man's an arrogant fool, like the rest. I've chosen my husband," Brianna smiled.

"He's no fool," Gabriel replied. "He spent most of the last jotnar war selling weapons to both sides."

Brianna laughed. "Then it is a very good thing that I have no intention of marrying him!"

"Brianna…" Gabriel looked at her from too far away. "What are you doing? If the Matriarch of the House announced your engagement, the deal has already been made. You can't change it."

"Perhaps not. But I cannot marry Cordov if I've already married you." Brianna crossed the room to slip her hands into his. "I've brought the rings that were made for me when I was a child," she hesitated, seeing the distant look in his eyes. "Have you changed your mind?"

Gabriel shook his head. "No. I haven't changed my mind. But making our promises now isn't going to convince them."

Brianna pulled the carved wooden box holding the rings out of her pocket. "But if we go back to the main house together, wearing my wedding rings, our promises will be sealed and they will be powerless." She held out one of the knotted gold rings.

Gabriel took the ring she offered. "No little bit of gold is going to stop a Matriarch of the Fae from doing whatever she pleases."

"It's not the gold, boy," Ardiel scolded his son. "Those are Fae rings. There's Power woven into every one of those knots."

"And once you're married, you become Madame Oreveille," Gabriel finished.

Brianna nodded. "Mother is ready to step down. These last years have been difficult for her. I am ready to take my place among the Matriarchs."

"Then form the circle," Gabriel replied.

Ardiel led them outside into the moonlight. Brianna traced a wide circle in the dust, and where she drew, the line began to glow. Around and around the circle she traced, making the line cross over and back again until it resembled the knotted gold of the Mark of Oreveille. Finally, she stood in the center of her circle and reached a hand across to Gabriel.

He took her hand and stepped across the glowing line in the dirt. As he joined her, the circle flared up, obscuring them as they whispered their promises to each other. Brianna opened her box and removed the second ring. Together, they held it up and the circle flared again as she slid it onto her finger.

Again, they held the second ring high and the circle flared with power. Gabriel hesitated for the briefest moment before sliding the ring onto his finger. Brianna watched as both rings glowed, their power complete. She felt the warmth of power brush her cheek as Gabriel reached for her, raised her face to his and claimed his bride within the glowing circle.

Several moments later, the circle dimmed. Ardiel stood, watching.

"There is one thing more we must do," Brianna whispered, not wanting to break the stillness of the circle.

She concentrated on the Sword of Oreveille, still concealed by the side of the house. It rose into the air and floated, once more glinting in the moonlight, into the circle. Brianna held out her hands, and the Sword came to rest across her palms.

"Master of Oreveille," she named her new husband.

"Madame," he returned the ritual greeting.

"It is your right to claim the title of Defender as well as Master of this House. Do you accept this title and the responsibility it carries, or will you name another?"

Gabriel held out his hands, palms bare. "I have defended the House of Oreveille against all threats, and I will continue. I am Defender of Oreveille."

Brianna smiled at his words. The Sword rose off her hands and righted itself before Gabriel. It hovered for a moment, as though judging his worth, before settling across his open palms. Brianna closed her eyes for a brief moment. It was done. Before she could speak, she felt a strange surge of power whip through the circle. When she opened her eyes again, Gabriel was staring into the darkness.

The Mark of the Sword glowed on his chest. Its brightness showed through the thin weave of his linen shirt. Brianna could see the outline of the sword, with the knotted gold woven around it. The Mark was similar to her own, close enough to recognize it as a Mark of Oreveille, but unmistakably his own.

"Gabriel," she whispered, touching his chest.

He held the Sword of Oreveille above his head in salute to the darkness he had been staring at, and put his free arm around her bare shoulders. The circle faded away, its power spent.

"What happened?" She asked.

"Your father gave me the Sword. Didn't you see him?"

Brianna shook her head. "He gave you more than the Sword," she added, tracing the outline of the Mark on his chest. "Unless I am wrong, he gave you power as well."

Ardiel stepped out of the shadows to embrace the couple. "I am happy for you both. Come back after you've done what you have to do at the main House, and we will celebrate."

CHAPTER THIRTEEN

Gabriel offered Brianna his arm. He knew this would only be the first of a long string of balls, so he might as well get used to them. It was a small price to pay to stand beside his Brianna instead of watching her bound with some worthless drunkard like her stepfather.

She did not speak as they walked up to the Great House, but the defiant tilt of her head and the pressure of her hand on his arm told him of her nervousness. He vowed not to cause her to regret her choice. He might be half-human, but he knew enough of the Fae and their ways to prove himself without embarrassing her.

As they approached the semi-circle stairs that led to the grand entrance, Brianna paused. Four footmen stood at attention, scanning the grounds.

"Mademoiselle D'Oreveille," one of the footmen spoke, the relief clear in his voice. "Madame has been searching for you."

Brianna nodded once. "You may announce that Madame Oreveille and her husband have arrived."

Gabriel put a hand over Brianna's, glancing down at her. He forced himself to looked away as the grand doors swung open. There would be plenty of time to lose himself in her green eyes after this evening was over.

Gabriel and Brianna walked slowly behind the footmen, waiting as they slid back the doors. The Matriarchs, their husbands, and their sons filled the room, sipping aperitifs and circulating, discussing the affairs of the Faeland, while the musicians played in the background.

"Madame... Oreveille," the footman hesitated as he announced Brianna. His companion had disappeared down the corridor.

For a second, all conversation stopped. Gabriel couldn't help but grin as he heard a young boy, perhaps nine or ten years old, giggle at the unfolding scene before his mother silenced him.

The crowd parted to allow Brianna's mother to pass. She stalked across the ballroom, stopping only inches from the couple.

"What do you think you are doing?" she hissed.

Brianna held out her hand. "You did invite us to dine with you this evening, Mother."

"Stupid girl. Do not presume to call yourself Madame. You are still the daughter of this house. Take that ring off your finger and put it away."

"No, Mother. I cannot." Brianna looked up, breaking the hushed exchange. She swept a glance around the room and announced, "Matriarchs of the Fae, may I present my husband, Gabriel of Oreveille!"

Gabriel stood motionless and met their gaze.

A moment of shocked silence passed, then the whispers began to grow. Speculation and assumptions began to bubble up almost instantly.

The sharp song of steel through air broke his concentration.

"Get out of my house, bastard human!" the old Master of Oreveille, Brianna's stepfather, swung again. Gabriel took a step back, grateful for the other man's love of brandy. It gave him a chance to draw the Sword of Oreveille to defend himself, deflecting the ornamental sabre.

Brianna and her mother stepped back to give the men room.

The old man swung again, leaving a long gash in Gabriel's waistcoat. Gabriel heard Brianna gasp as the hot blood seeped through. He felt the cold steel break through his skin, but he had no time to react. He could smell the brandy seeping from his opponent's pores as he stumbled forward, swinging wildly at Gabriel's face.

"One thrust, and Oreveille is yours." Gabriel glanced up as heard the voice echo through his mind. Cordov met his eyes and nodded.

"Sit down, old man," Gabriel held out the sword, hoping to end the fight. He did not wish to shed blood on his wedding night.

"Or you let the drunkard kill you, and I will marry the D'Oreveille."

Gabriel thrust the Sword of Oreveille to push the old man back. As he did so, Brianna's stepfather rushed forward. Gabriel fell to one knee, ducking the man's flailing sword. If he could get close enough, he could easily wrench the blade from the old man's hand.

Gabriel felt a weight on his sword, and looked up to see the other man's sallow skin and faded, dull hair fallen over his panicked eyes. His full attention was focused on the sword between his ribs. It left him no energy for maintaining glamour.

Someone screamed as body of the Master of Oreveille slid to the floor.

"Murderer!" Cordov's voice broke through the shocked paralysis of the room. Before he could stand, Gabriel was surrounded by more Fae than he could count. His hands were wrenched behind his back, and a sword was held to his throat. One of the half-Fae footmen reached for the Sword of Oreveille. The moment his fingertips brushed the steel, Gabriel could feel power arcing through the Sword to throw him back.

The footman screamed and stumbled back from the sword. Gabriel could hear Madame Oreveille's furiously silent voice as she demanded answers from Brianna.

"What did you do?"

Brianna smiled. "I did nothing, Mother. You know that the Sword protects itself against thieves. No Fae man may touch it unless he is the sworn Defender of Oreveille."

"The Sword has not been bound since the death of your father. It cannot be bound again."

"And yet Gabriel held the Sword in salute not two hours ago."

"And he dies in the morning."

"Let him go!" Brianna commanded the footmen.

"You see what happens when you bring a bastard human into the house?" her mother spoke aloud. "They cause nothing but chaos. Lock the human in the slave cells for the night. This is, after all, a party. I will deal with his execution in the morning," she commanded, reasserting her place as Mistress of the House.

"Let him go!" Brianna screamed, fighting her way through the crowd. Gabriel wished he had some small measure of his father's ability to walk with the spirits, so he could tell her not to worry, but all he could do was try to catch a last glimpse of her as the Fae propelled him out the doors, giving the Sword a wide berth.

Tricia Ballad

CHAPTER FOURTEEN

Brianna stood and watched her stepfather choke out his last gurgled breath, and fought the urge to kick him. Her Gabriel was locked somewhere in the bowels of the house. In the morning, he would die for the old man's stupidity.

She looked up at the faces of her mother's friends and allies. Already, they had gone back to their wine and rumors, as though this had been nothing more than a shocking play put on for their entertainment. Her mother directed the footmen who carried the dead man out of the ballroom and cleaned the puddle of blood left behind.

Brianna stood and watched until there was no sign that she had brought Gabriel into this ballroom, less than an hour ago. Her mother hovered nearby with Madame Dechaund, giving Brianna no chance to slip away again.

"Brianna," Cordov appeared at her elbow. "Some wine, perhaps?" She took the glass he offered, wondering how the orchestra could still play, while the servants prepared the Master of the House for burial, and her Gabriel awaited execution.

Madame Oreveille joined them, her face devoid of any sign of fury or grief. "Dreadfully exciting moment, no?"

Cordov raised his glass. "Situations can change without a moment's notice, Madame."

"They can," Madame Oreveille smiled. "Would you care to dance?"

Relieved, Brianna handed her untouched wine to a servant. If only Cordov would keep her mother occupied for several dances, she might have a chance to think.

She watched, mesmerized, as her mother and Cordov swirled through the dancing couples. Their heads were close together in whispered confidence. Brianna began to regret giving up her wine.

At last the guests began to leave, Brianna made her excuses as well, but Madame Oreveille shook her head.

"Stay a moment, Brianna. You have a duty to perform." Brianna's stomach clenched at her mother's cold tone.

Madame Oreveille led her into a small antechamber. Madame Dechaund and Cordov waited within. Brianna searched, but their faces revealed nothing.

"Thanks to your childish willfulness, Oreveille is without a Master. I had intended a proper Fae wedding for you, but under the circumstances..."

"I am already married, Mother. Or had you forgotten?" Brianna interrupted.

"Whatever you have done with your human is of no consequence," Madame Oreveille snapped. The room was charged as she regained her composure.

"As I was saying, the jotnar raids have become more common. We have had three - or is it four? - slave escapes this month. We simply cannot leave Oreveille without a Master while you play and flirt and reject every young man in the Faeland!"

"Oreveille has both a Master and a Defender," Brianna spoke quietly.

"Stop with this nonsense, Brianna. You will marry Cordov, and introduce him as Master of Oreveille in the morning."

"I will not. I cannot. This evening, I married Gabriel within the knotted circle. We are bound by the power of that circle and the rings we both wear. Even you cannot break a soul-binding, Mother."

Brianna stood under her mother's searching gaze. She watched the anger and frustration in her eyes as the older woman probed her memories.

"You stupid, stupid child," Madame Oreveille whispered.

"Perhaps not all is lost," Madame Dechaund spoke from the shadows. "An alliance between our houses is still possible, even without the cooperation of the girl."

Madame Oreveille turned, a smile breaking her lips. "Yes. You are right, of course. Our agreement did not specify which Matriarch of Oreveille should bring your House onto the council."

"Exactly, Madame," Cordov stepped forward, offering his hand to Madame Oreveille.

"Very well," Madame Oreveille swept a triumphant smile toward Brianna. "As you are all witnesses, I declare Cordov Dechaund shall hereby be known as Cordov, husband and Master of the House of Oreveille!"

Cordov bowed low over Madame Oreveille's hand. "It is an honor, Madame."

"Master of Oreveille," Madame returned the greeting.

Brianna stood still, watching the impromptu wedding. Her mind raced, as she adjusted to this development. Her mother would keep her seat on the Council of Matriarchs, and retain control of Oreveille. Brianna would remain the Daughter of the House. But what of Gabriel?

Brianna had no answer as she left the chamber.

In the garden, her mind finally began to clear. She needed to be in the open air to think, to plan. Whatever else happened on this night, she would not allow Gabriel to die. She had to get him out of the slave cell before dawn. If she waited until they brought him out, it would be too late. If she could only get down into the cellars, she could manipulate the metal locks, but surely they would have guards posted.

Brianna clenched her fists in frustration. There had to be a way!

An hour later, she returned to the house. Pacing in the garden was not going to free Gabriel. As she climbed the wide staircase, she took note of the servants. They would be occupied for the next few hours removing all signs of her mother's impromptu ball.

In her chamber, Brianna waited, listening to the voices in the air. Once the house was completely still, she floated noiselessly down corridors and staircases to the cellar.

Brianna paused at the bottom of the cellar stairs to allow her eyes to adjust to the darkness. As she expected, two men sat outside the slave cell. Brianna smiled. While her mother may have instructed the Fae footmen to guard Gabriel, they had obviously found a pair of humans to take their place.

"Come with me. I'll get you back to Gaia." Brianna heard Gabriel whisper.

The two human men hesitated.

"All you have to do is unlock the cell and I'll take you with me. I know the way out of the Faeland," Gabriel whispered again.

"We don't have the keys," one of the humans replied.

Brianna stepped forward. "I can unlock the doors."

"Bri?" Gabriel's voice came though the darkness.

"We have to hurry," Brianna replied as she sent her awareness into the open spaces in the lock. She felt the mechanism and slowly slid it into place. The door swung open.

Gabriel was at her side in an instant, his lips pressed to hers.

Brianna wrapped her arms around him, and felt the sticky drying blood through his shirt. In the dim light she could see the Mark of the Sword outlined on his chest, broken by ripped flesh. She touched the wound, sending her spirit into the body of her husband. So much pain. A jagged shard of steel lay scraping against his beating heart. Every move ripped more flesh, spilled more blood.

Brianna gasped. His injuries were far beyond her skill. He would surely die if he moved, but if he stayed, her mother would have him hanged.

She pulled at the metal shard. Perhaps, if she could remove it, then patch the ripped flesh and torn muscle...

She began to pull it away from his heart, only to jam it against his rib. She tried to wiggle it out, but only seemed to do more damage.

"Please, just move!" she begged, wishing Madame Riet were here. She stopped, feeling his entire being from within. Perhaps he was strong enough to move, now that the shard was not against his heart. She could try again to remove it once they reached the safety of Gaia.

Brianna opened her eyes, looking at Gabriel. He stared at her, but did not ask questions.

"Come!" Brianna insisted.

Gabriel turned to the two guards. "Now's your only chance. Are you coming, or will you stay here and face the Fae?"

"You've given us little choice," one of them accused. "If we stay here, we'll die for this."

"Then let's go," Gabriel took the Sword of Oreveille and led the way further into the cellar, to an old delivery door. "We have to get my father. He knows the way to Gaia."

Brianna silently slid the old door open. The cool night air welcomed them.

"Hurry!" she whispered. "We must be gone before morning!"

Gabriel led the way through the darkness to the slave village. His father's cottage was dark, but as they approached they could see the older man standing outside holding a satchel.

"I'm glad to see you, boy," he said as the group came near. "But I didn't expect you to bring half the party."

"It's Brianna's doing, Da. She sprang the locks. These two are humans, set to guard duty tonight. They didn't raise the alarm, the least we can do is take them home."

Gabriel's father stood. "You've made a hard choice for us all, killing the master of the house," he said.

Gabriel looked his father in the eye, grateful the old man had talent in spirit walking. It saved precious time. "I didn't mean to kill him. He lurched onto my sword. If he had been sober, he might have..."

He did not give his son a chance to finish. "You'll have time later to worry about what might have been. Now we must get to the docks, and cross over while we still can. They'll be searching, and this is the first place they'll look."

He grabbed his satchel. "Have you any coin, girl?" he asked.

Brianna nodded. "A few gold pieces. Not much," she answered.

"It will do to buy us a room at the village inn if need be. Now let's go." The old man led the way out of the cottage toward the beach beyond. Gabriel kept hold of Brianna's hand, guiding her through the darkness, as the humans followed.

CHAPTER FIFTEEN

At the docks, Gabriel's father led them resolutely toward one of the cutters kept for coastal defense.

"Get those sails up!" he ordered as he untied the ropes securing the small ship to the mooring. Brianna stood on deck, unsure of what he wanted her to do. The men ignored her as they worked to bring the ship out of the harbor.

Gabriel, his father, and the two human men adjusted the sails and changed course several times over the next several hours. Brianna's eyes adjusted to the darkness, but she still could not see more than a few feet ahead. It seemed as though they sailed in circles, yet without any sort of landmarks on the bare ocean, she could not be sure. Gabriel was too busy with the sails to reassure her, and his father seemed to know the route. In the end, all Brianna could do was to find a corner of the small ship and wait.

She watched Gabriel carefully, but he showed no signs of pain or fatigue. She realized that she had not experienced sense of emptiness when she pulled her spirit out of his body, as she had when Madame Riet pulled her out of the flower. Perhaps it was simply because they had to hurry, and she hadn't had time to feel anything.

At last, their strange circular path ended at a roughly built wooden dock. The beach was deserted, though Brianna could see a few telltale wisps of smoke rising out of the trees nearby. Gabriel's father motioned for them to wait out of sight while he watched and listened at the dirt path that led from the beach into the forest. The way seemed deserted and silent, and he waved the young couple and the two human guards forward.

"Are we...?" Brianna began. The old man nodded. "This is the way to the human lands," he turned to the two men. "I thank you for your help this night. You are back in your own world."

The two looked at each other, nodded their thanks to Ardiel, and took off into the forest.

Ardiel waited until they were gone, then concentrated for a long moment. Brianna watched as his appearance changed. His skin faded to a dull tan, and his hair darkened from the sheen of burnished copper to resemble the color of rust.

"Now you," The old man nodded to Brianna.

Brianna recalled her lessons in glamour, learned when she was just a little girl. She conjured up the image of herself, then dulled the vibrant black shine of her hair, and dampened the glow in her eyes. She softened the pearlescent glow of her skin until it was gone. Finally, the Mark of Oreveille, which she had worn since her birth, to fade. She turned to Gabriel. "Do I look like a proper human wife?" she asked, hoping he would approve of her new appearance, yet afraid he would be repulsed by it. She had never thought to use glamour to make herself ugly.

Gabriel looked at her for a long moment. "You are beautiful as always, Bri. No magic will ever hide that."

She smiled at him and took his arm.

"Remember, there are different rules here, girl," the old man reminded Brianna. "You'd best get used to deferring to your husband, not the other way 'round."

"Truly? I thought that was simply a story told to frighten young girls who got too adventurous," Brianna exclaimed.

"Aye. 'Tis the truth. You know how to cook?" he asked.

"Cook?" Brianna echoed.

The old man did not reply, but spent the next hour muttering about foolish children as they walked along the dirt road.

Tricia Ballad

CHAPTER SIXTEEN

It was nearly morning when they saw the first wisps of smoke from the village chimneys. By the grey dawn light, Brianna thought she saw something like hope on the old man's face.

He walked into the small village, and went directly to a small house at the very center of the community. It had been a sweet home once, and was badly in need of repair. The little space between the gate and the front door was carefully tended, however, and devoted to growing vegetables and herbs.

The old man stopped outside the garden gate. "I'll find out if Kathleen is still here," he said to Brianna, "if you'll watch over me on this side of the mists?"

Brianna nodded. She had performed this service many times for other spirit walkers. When their consciousness entered the spirit realm, it left their physical bodies completely abandoned and vulnerable.

Brianna looked up at Gabriel. His mouth struggled between hope and dread at the name of his mother, who had disappeared when he was just four years old. Before she could say anything of comfort, the old man opened his eyes.

"She's here, and she's alone. I asked her to come out – we'll see if she heard me," he said.

Several long moments later, a woman of middle age opened the door. She gripped a light shawl around her shoulders. Brianna caught a glimpse of her bare feet beneath her skirts. The woman glanced, first one direction, then the other, down the street that ran past her door. At first she did not seem to notice the tiny group outside her garden gate. After assuring herself that her neighbors were all still in bed, she dared a look at them.

"Is it truly you?" She asked, barely above a whisper.

"Aye, Kathleen. It is. May we come in? We've stories to tell," Ardiel answered.

The woman stepped back into the shadows of her little house to allow them entrance. She lit several candles, giving the room a soft, welcoming glow.

"You've visited me every night since we parted, but I'd long since given up hope that you would come to take me home," she said to the old man.

"And still I cannot," he said. "My life is forfeit by now in the Faeland, for helping these two escape."

Kathleen looked at Gabriel and Brianna. "And what crime have you committed, children?" she asked.

Brianna began to speak, but Gabriel was quicker. "I am a thief. I stole the heart of the D'Oreveille."

Brianna smiled at the truth of his words.

Kathleen looked closely at Brianna. "The Daughter of Oreveille?" Brianna nodded. "And was your heart truly stolen, or given freely as a gift?"

"This man is all I could ever desire. He has won my heart many times over. I will have no other," Brianna declared. "He is no thief. If anything, I am the thief, for I stole the jewel of the estate and two of the villa's best men besides."

"And why have you brought this band of thieves to my door?" Kathleen asked the old man, laughing.

"Because he is your son," Ardiel spoke quietly.

"My little Gabriel?" Kathleen whispered.

Ardiel nodded.

Kathleen looked at her son proudly. "You were hardly more than a baby…but of course you have grown. It has been so many long years…" she spoke to herself as much as to her son. "You have raised him to be a good man, Ardiel. Just like his father," she smiled.

"Good day, Mother," Gabriel spoke the unfamiliar words.

Kathleen opened her arms to embrace her son. "A very good day, my son. A very good day." When she finally released him, she turned to Brianna. "And you, jewel of Oreveille…"

Gabriel offered his hand to Brianna. "Mother, this is Brianna D'Oreveille. We played together as children, and we married last night."

"Are you quite certain of your choice, my girl?" Kathleen asked. "Surely you know that there are very good reasons for Fae and humans to remain apart." She smiled at Ardiel, and beckoned to him to sit with her at the table.

"But Gabriel is half-Fae," Brianna insisted. "And besides, I would prefer a single year with him to a thousand centuries with any of Fae man of my generation."

Kathleen smiled. "But are you prepared to live as a human wife? Do you know what that means?" she continued.

Brianna nodded. "I will learn if you will teach me what I need to know."

"And are you prepared to go on living when he dies?" Kathleen pressed.

Brianna stilled. "I will do what I must. I will have my life with Gabriel, and when it is over, I will return to the Faeland and bury my grief in politics. Or perhaps I will stay here and be a grandmother and a wise woman."

"I will do what I must," she repeated, "until I can join him in the mists."

"You must be careful. The Fae are not well liked here. People fear what they do not understand. A man who lives in fear soon lashes out at the thing that terrifies him," she warned.

"I will live as an ordinary human woman, and hide all sign of what I am. I promise!" Brianna spoke earnestly. "Will you help us?"

"I lost my son once, I will not turn him away now, simply because he has chosen a Fae bride. I only pray it does not cost you as dearly as it cost me."

Gabriel looked down at Brianna, whose eyes shined with the tears she knew she would shed one day. "Aye. You must go on living. I will return to you, Bri. Even if the Matriarchs would pretend otherwise, I do have Fae blood in my veins. My spirit will always find you, no matter what body it finds itself in."

"Are you asking me to place my hopes in an old legend?" Brianna asked incredulously.

"Legends carry truth in them, and it's a truth you'll need to carry you through the dark years," Kathleen reminded her.

Brianna nodded. "Then I will carry the legends in my heart – and interrogate every man I meet after your death," she laughed, standing on tiptoe to seal her promise with a kiss.

Tricia Ballad

CHAPTER SEVENTEEN

Early the next morning, Kathleen pulled her shawl more tightly around her shoulders against the early morning chill, and went to bring a bucket of water in from the village well. While she was gone, Brianna explored the tiny cottage. The main room held all the implements of daily life that she would soon learn to use. The hearth was cold and dark, but the firewood stacked neatly nearby suggested that it would warm the entire house. She picked up two small logs and set them on the floor of the hearth, working out how to light the fire. If she could but have the fire started when Kathleen returned, perhaps that would convince the older woman that she would not be completely useless.

Gabriel knelt beside her at the hearth. "Like this," he said, placing a third log in the hearth and arranging them in a triangle. He pulled a handful of kindling out of the basket beside the logs, tucked it underneath. Finally, he dug an ember from the previous night's fire out of the banked ashes at the back of the hearth and used it to light the kindling. Brianna watched the process intently.

"Blow on the embers to get them to light," Gabriel instructed. "There's a bit of a knack to it," he admitted, as she tried and only succeeded in blowing out the delicate red glow. He pulled another ember from the ashes and lit the fire for her.

Kathleen returned a few moments later. She smiled when she saw her son and Brianna sitting before the cheerful little fire, their fingers intertwined. "Good morning, children," she greeted them. "Brianna, perhaps you would like to join me in the village today? I need a few things from the market, then I will show you how to find the healing herbs I use from the forest."

After a simple breakfast, Brianna walked with Kathleen down the dirt road that led into the village. She felt strangely self-conscious in the plain cotton gown Kathleen had lent her. She understood. Her purple silk would attract as much attention in the small human village as the Mark of Oreveille. Brianna glanced at the older woman for reassurance. It had taken Brianna most of an hour to fade the Glamour of that Mark, and if she lost concentration, it was likely to reappear.

As they approached the village, a young man ran toward them. He stopped before Kathleen, struggling to catch his breath.

"Darron! Slow down. Is it Cara?" Kathleen asked the young man, gathering all she needed to know from the look of desperation in his eyes.

The young man nodded. "She's been laboring all night, but the baby won't come. Her ma is with her. There's so much blood," he choked out the simple phrases that hinted at his worst fear.

Kathleen nodded. "I'll come. Brianna, this may be difficult. If you would like to return to the house, we can do our shopping another time."

"No. I have studied a bit of healing. I may be able to help," Brianna appealed to Kathleen.

The older woman looked at her sharply.

"Please, hurry!" Darron pleaded.

Kathleen let out a quick breath. "An extra set of hands will be welcome." She and Brianna followed the young man into the village, rushing to keep up with him.

Brianna heard the laboring woman's screams as they approached the small cottage. Darron waited in the garden, helpless, while the two women went inside. In the darkened room, Brianna saw the woman struggling to give birth. Her eyes were vacant, as though she saw nothing but the pain. She was young, perhaps sixteen. Hardly old enough to marry and bear a child! Brianna wondered if it was common for human girls to marry so young. Perhaps, given their shortened lives, it was important for them to grow up quickly.

"Brianna!" Kathleen's voice interrupted her musings. "Hold her hands. I have to try to turn the baby. It will be painful, but she must lie still or she could injure herself or the baby."

Brianna nodded and went to the girl's side. Taking her hands, she spoke soft, soothing words, hoping to distract her from the pain. As she spoke, she watched Kathleen in fascination. The older woman worked for a quarter of an hour before shaking her head.

"The cord is knotted around the baby's neck. I can't turn the little one without choking it."

Brianna closed her eyes and sent her Spirit into the young woman's writhing body. She saw the baby girl, stuck at the top of the birth canal, her hips too wide to fit through. She saw the cord, just as Kathleen had described it, in a loose knot around the baby's neck. She felt the pain as the mother's body desperately convulsed, trying to deliver her baby.

Brianna felt the pulsing cord. Perhaps, if she could undo the knot... this would not be so different from the healing she performed on Gabriel. She felt the cord again, floating in fluid. She pushed, tentative at first, to see if she could move the thick strands. Carefully, she untangled the rope and slipped it over the infant's head.

A rush of exhilaration pulsed through her mind. Next was to turn her, so her head would fit into her mother's pelvis. Now that the cord was untangled, nudging her into position was easy. She floated, ready to be born.

"Brianna!" Kathleen's sharp voice hissed in her ear. Brianna opened her eyes, disoriented in the dimly lit room. The crackling fire competed for her attention with the laboring girl's moans. She felt the hard wooden floor, although she did not recall sitting down. Someone had draped a coarse woolen blanket over her head and shoulders. She was grateful for it; despite the fire, the room felt cold. Kathleen shook her head, her eyes wide with alarm.

"The girl has never attended a birth - the blood must have frightened her." Brianna heard Kathleen's voice, although she could not grasp her meaning.

"The baby…" Brianna began, trying to reassure her that the infant would be born safely.

A triumphant scream cut her short. Kathleen turned to the mother in time to guide the infant girl into the world, and Brianna smiled as she heard the child's answering wail.

At once, the room erupted into frantic activity as the older women finished the age-old rituals of childbirth. The placenta was delivered, the cord cut and tied, and the newly washed infant was laid at her mother's breast. Through all of this, Brianna stayed back, watching and learning. This was a new sort of power, born of action. So different from what she learned from Madame Riet!

Someone thrust a pile of bloody linens into Brianna's arms. "Go get these soaking, girl," the woman instructed, pointing toward a basin of steaming water. Brianna nodded wordlessly, but the woman had already moved on to other tasks.

Brianna recoiled from the filthy linens as she shoved them into the soapy water. She looked around the room -

surely there was a servant whose job it was to erase all of the blood and dirt, and return the linens, neatly folded, to their closet! But even as the thought formed, Brianna knew it was absurd. This was not Oreveille. Here, on Gaia, she was not the Powerful daughter of any House. Here she was simply Brianna, wife of Gabriel, an ordinary man. She smiled at the thought. Gabriel was anything but ordinary, on either side of the pathways!

Recalling her task, Brianna tensed, but forced her hands to push the linens back into the pink and grey suds. The water stung but she continued, not knowing what else to do. At least she was no longer cold.

At last, the room was clean and mother and child rested peacefully. Kathleen touched Brianna's shoulders, removing the forgotten blanket. "Gabriel and Ardiel will wonder why we are late. We should get home." Brianna nodded as the older woman led her outside.

Once they were well down the road, Kathleen turned to Brianna. "Why did you not heed my warnings?"

Brianna looked into the other woman's face, but saw nothing but worry and irritation. "I had to do something! They were both going to die."

"You lost control, and your whole body glowed. The Mark of your House was brightest of all. I only hope I was able to cover you before the other women noticed." Kathleen walked faster.

Brianna hurried to keep up. "I am sorry, I did not realize the Mark would appear so brightly if I stopped focusing on my Glamour for a moment." She let out a frustrated breath. "Would you have me let them both die?"

"Do you know what they will do if one of them saw you?" Kathleen stopped and turned to Brianna.

"They will be fearful, I suppose. They will not trust me," Brianna answered.

"They will accuse you of witchcraft, of consorting with devils and demons and all manner of evil. Have you not heard the stories?" Kathleen asked.

Brianna shook her head. She had heard rumors and hysterical tales from some of the more militant Houses, ones who wished to invade and civilize Gaia. For the human's own good, they always claimed. She had long ago dismissed the tales of mobs burning innocent Fae in the town square as nothing more than inflammatory rhetoric. But now Kathleen, Gabriel's mother, who knew as much as anyone about both sides of the pathways, seemed truly afraid.

"One whispered rumor that you did not seem quite normal, and that the infant lived when it should have died, and they will have all the evidence they need to convict us both as witches." Kathleen took Brianna's arm and kept walking toward her cottage. "It is not worth risking the flames. We must go, find somewhere else, and start again."

"Flames?" Brianna kept her voice low, although she could not see anyone about.

"That is what they do with a convicted witch, if she survives their interrogations. They tie her to a pole and light a bonfire at her feet. If she is lucky, she chokes to death on the smoke before the flames reach her body." Kathleen walked faster.

Brianna was silent as she checked her appearance, reassuring herself that all signs of her Fae nature were well hidden. She hurried to catch up to Kathleen. They walked silently the rest of the way to the small cottage on the edge of the village.

CHAPTER EIGHTEEN

The following morning was quiet and tense, as reality descended. Kathleen guided Brianna in preparing a simple breakfast of bread, cheese, and wine mixed with water.

"Gabriel and I will go into the village to find work," Ardiel announced, as they sat down to eat.

"Many of the farmers have been hiring day laborers to help with planting," Kathleen offered. "They tend to gather outside the tavern in the morning, and return there to pay wages in the evening."

Gabriel watched Brianna as she ate. She maintained her human disguise, even when they alone. Somehow that bothered him. He understood how necessary it was for her to appear human and ordinary, but it seemed to take so much of her energy. He hoped it would get easier for her as the days passed.

"Be careful," Kathleen added as Ardiel and Gabriel finished their meal. "And listen for rumors. They will be our best warning."

Gabriel glanced again at Brianna, hoping to reassure her, but she kept her eyes on her food and did not look up. She had not spoken a word this morning, though she had plenty to say the night before, when Kathleen told them how she assisted with the birth. Then, Brianna had been certain that she could cope with any threat, but today she seemed less sure.

Kathleen stood as well. "I need to visit Cara and the baby. I will walk into town with you."

Brianna looked up at the girl's name. "Should I...?" she left the question hanging in the air.

Kathleen shook her head. "Why don't you stay here and rest? So much has happened in the last few days. Some quiet time to yourself might help restore your spirits."

Brianna's shoulders sagged but she nodded. "I'll try," she agreed.

Gabriel walked around the table to sit next to Brianna. "Rest," he echoed. "Kathleen is right, you'll feel better for some quiet. I'll be back this evening."

Brianna looked up, and Gabriel could see the worry in her eyes. He kissed her, lingering at her lips for longer than he intended, wishing he could erase the concerns that darkened her eyes and silenced her voice.

"Everything will be fine. I'll see you tonight," he whispered against her dark hair as she clung to him.

Tricia Ballad

CHAPTER NINETEEN

Brianna sat at the long wooden table and watched as the three important people in her life left her behind in the tiny cottage. The room was silent. After several long moments, Brianna looked around. Both Gabriel and Kathleen had advised her to rest, but she could not simply close her eyes and wander into the mists of a dream. She was too agitated. She was accustomed to leisure, but not to boredom. At home, she filled her days with study and rides across the island on her favorite horse. Here, Kathleen had made it clear that she was to stay indoors, but what was there to do in this tiny cottage? She could not even practice her studies, lest some snooping neighbor pass by and accuse her of witchcraft!

She stood up. Perhaps she could at least tidy up after breakfast. This was the sort of thing human wives were expected to do, she supposed. And it would pass the time until Kathleen returned.

An hour later, the breakfast dishes were cleared away and washed as well as Brianna could do them, and the floor was swept. Brianna sat back down, and once again the silence engulfed her. She looked out the window, hoping to see Kathleen walking down the dirt road. Brianna turned away in disappointment to face the empty room.

Her glance fell on the Sword of Oreveille, set in the corner of the room the night they arrived on Gaia.

Brianna's thoughts were interrupted by a knock at the door. She paused, fixing the illusion of human appearance in her mind. When she was satisfied that she had erased all sign of her Fae nature, she opened the door.

A rough-looking man of middle years stood on the doorstep. His greasy hair hung in tangled grey strands across his face.

"Is the midwife at home?" he asked, looking beyond Brianna into the cottage.

Brianna shook her head. "No, she has gone to see a girl in the village. Is there something wrong?"

The man looked carefully at Brianna for a long moment before stepping back into the garden. "I'll find her in the village then," he answered, taking another look into the cottage before he left.

Brianna closed the door, hoping he believed her to be nothing more than an ordinary human wife.

CHAPTER TWENTY

Gabriel was no stranger to hard labor. He had worked in the fields alongside human slaves from the time he was old enough to haul the heavy bundles of sugarcane back to the wagons. This day's work had been something very different. In the Faeland, he was the overseer's son, and while he did his share of the work, he did not feel the sting of the lash when he paused to rest his aching muscles before moving on to the next row.

His body ached and his temper simmered as the overseer dropped two silver coins into his chapped and bloody hand outside the village tavern.

"Come inside, have a drink to cool off," Ardiel guided Gabriel into the dark building and ordered two tankards of ale.

Gabriel swallowed the bitter liquid, forcing himself to relax. It had been a hard day; that was all. He thought of Brianna, and wondered how she had fared on her first full day on Gaia. She had been so silent this morning. He had never seen her afraid before. But then, he realized, she had never been to a place where her Power and position were less than useless.

"Aye, a sword of uncommon beauty and strength. It's been stolen, and my master has sent me to find it, and bring the thief to justice."

Gabriel looked up from his ale. A man spoke to the tavern keeper. He wore a powdered wig and elaborate frockcoat like a man accustomed to finery but not the leisure that usually accompanied it.

"How do we know this sword belongs to your master? There are any number of good swords about," the tavern keeper answered.

"It is inscribed with the sigil of my master's clan, and the legend, 'Defender of Oreveille'" the man replied, pulling a scrap of paper out of his pocket to show to the tavern keeper. He turned to the room, holding the drawing high. "My master has offered a generous reward to any man who returns this precious sword and delivers the thief to him," he announced.

At first, there was only whispered speculation of the stranger's reward as the drawing was passed around the room. As the minutes passed, Gabriel and his father finished their ale, watching the stranger and listening to the rumors being birthed all around them.

Gabriel closed his eyes. His head began to swim, as though he had drank more than he should, and when he opened his eyes again, he saw the stranger at the wheel of a great ship. He was dressed somewhat better than his crew, and gave orders in rapid succession. Even onboard ship, he wore that perfectly curled and powdered wig. As the wind began to blow, the sails opened up and the ship moved out of harbor. The man at the wheel smiled triumphantly, thinking of the gold his master would surely pay for the cargo he held below. The man urged the wind to blow harder, and his hair began to loose from its artfully designed curls. It was no wig, Gabriel realized. The man was Fae, or half-Fae at least! He bore no House Mark on his brow, and his skin was as brown as Gabriel's but his hair held the same brilliant luster, and he could command the Air.

"Come on, boy. It's time we got back," Ardiel's voice broke through Gabriel's vision, bringing him out of the mists and back to the darkened tavern. The well-dressed stranger was deep in conversation, listening to an old man with greasy silver hair telling tales of the village midwife.

"She's a witch-woman, as sure as anything," the old man insisted. "And that girl she took in is worse. You know my granddaughter was birthing just last night, and the baby was dead, they said. But the witch-woman and her girl came and the girl fell into a dream, and what do you know but the baby was born as alive as anything."

Gabriel nodded. He did not know who this half-Fae man was, or how he had followed them, but it was only a matter of time before he sought out the newest residents of the village.

The strange man motioned to the tavern keeper for another round of ale. The old villager nodded his thanks and went on with his story.

"So this morning I went there to get the truth of things, and the midwife was gone but the girl was there. Strangest girl I ever saw! Something not quite right about that girl, but I couldn't quite tell what. She told me the midwife was out, and what do you know but when I looked into the cottage, there was a fine looking sword propped up in the corner. Might just be the one you're looking for…"

Gabriel drained his ale.

CHAPTER TWENTY-ONE

As soon as they left the tavern, Ardiel stopped. "You go back to the cottage. Get Brianna and whatever supplies you can. I'll go find Kathleen."

Gabriel nodded. "I'll meet you on the beach where we landed. The ship is still there."

"Be careful. If we are not there in one hour, you and Brianna sail."

Gabriel did not reply. He would not abandon his father, or the mother he had so recently found, to whatever passed for justice in this corner of Gaia. Instead he forced himself to walk calmly down the dirt road toward Kathleen's cottage, so as not to raise the suspicions of anyone who might happen to glance his way.

At last, he reached the cottage door, and slipped inside. Brianna sat, rocking, her eyes softly vacant.

"Bri?" he spoke softly, unwilling to disturb her peace any more than necessary. She had wrapped a quilt around her head and shoulders, but he could see the glow of the Mark of Oreveille on her forehead.

He knelt before her and took her hands, but she did not respond. Gabriel wondered how long she had spent in this deep elemental trance.

"Brianna!" He tried again to rouse her, but she did not respond.

He concentrated on her face. He had fallen into the mists in the tavern, perhaps he could do it again. Once again, he felt the disorienting sense of floating, and saw Brianna floating through a brilliantly blue sky.

"Brianna!" he called silently, and she whirled around to face him.

"Gabriel? How are you here?" she asked, suddenly beside him.

"I do not know. But we must hurry. There is a half-Fae man here, looking for the Sword of Oreveille and the thief who stole it."

"Who is he?"

"I do not know. He appears human, except for his pearl white hair. He did not bear the Mark of any House. Hurry!"

Brianna raised his hand to her lips. Gabriel noticed that the bloody scratches from the day were gone.

Reluctantly, Gabriel opened his eyes. Brianna blinked in the dim light.

"We must hurry," Gabriel repeated. She stood and began to gather what food she could. Gabriel wrapped the sword in her quilt, and looked around the tiny cottage for any other provisions they might require.

Half an hour later, they left the cottage with their bundles. "We'll go this way," Gabriel pointed toward the dense forest that surrounded the village. Down the road, he could already see a crowd milling at the edge of the road leading toward Kathleen's cottage.

Picking their way through the jungle undergrowth was slow, but safer than meeting up with men enflamed by the promise of more gold than they had ever seen.

Finally, they made their way around the village to the house where only a day before Brianna had helped save two lives. From their hiding place, Gabriel could hear the strong, healthy cries of the infant. He smiled. Without his Brianna and her Power, this house would have been somber and quiet today.

"Wait here," Gabriel whispered. "I'll go see if they are here."

"No," Brianna put a hand on his arm. "Wait."

Gabriel looked again and saw a crowd of about twenty men advancing on the house, led by the old man with the greasy hair.

"I tell you, the midwife is a witch-woman!" he screamed over the din of the crowd. "And sure as not, she has this good man's sword, stolen for its magic power!"

Brianna gripped Gabriel's arm tighter.

The mob shouted its agreement.

"She is in there right now, doing God knows what to my innocent granddaughter and her baby!" The old man ranted.

The door to the house opened, and Ardiel stepped outside. Gabriel let out a breath. If any man could talk sense into this mob, it was his father.

"Gentlemen!" Ardiel's voice rose over the roar of the impatient crowd. "Kathleen has lived among you these twenty years, and not one of you can name a single injury she has caused."

"This man's sword! She has stolen his master's sword!" came a voice from the crowd.

"How has she stolen anything? She has been right here in this village, among you, every day." Ardiel answered.

The crowd pressed forward into the garden, demanding Kathleen and the witch-girl.

Gabriel unwrapped the Sword, ready to lurch forward. He could not crouch here, hiding in the forest, while his mother was taken from him again.

"Run!" Ardiel's voice rang loud in Gabriel's ears. He looked up, but his father did not so much as glance in his direction.

"You heard him too," Brianna whispered.

"Do you know what that mob will do to her?"

"Gabriel. Look - they are already through the door. They will do what they will do," Brianna's grip on his arm was harder than he expected. "You came to me in the mists. Go to her that way! You can guide Kathleen's spirit, so that she will not feel a single moment of their torture."

Gabriel watched as the mob emerged from the house. Four men held Ardiel as he fought. Several others surrounded Kathleen as though they were afraid to touch her.

"Where is the sword, witch-woman?" The greasy-haired old man demanded.

Kathleen did not answer.

"Where is the girl who worked spells on my granddaughter?"

Still no answer. Kathleen's eyes seemed fixed on a distant horizon.

"Answer, witch-woman!" The mob grew more and more agitated as Kathleen refused to acknowledge them.

"Run, Gabriel! Kathleen and I go into the mists, where we will be together. Go!" Ardiel's voice boomed in Gabriel's mind.

"Goodbye, Mother," Gabriel sent the thought toward Kathleen.

"Farewell, my little Gabriel. Be happy," came his mother's voice.

"I will hold them off as long as I can," Ardiel promised. "Be happy."

Gabriel looked at Brianna. Her tear-filled eyes told him that she had heard the brief exchange.

"They will feel no pain, and will be happy together," she whispered, clinging to his arm.

Gabriel nodded, concealing the Sword once again. He led the way back through the dense growth toward the beach.

Tricia Ballad

CHAPTER TWENTY-TWO

Brianna watched the sun rise over the Eastern horizon of the Caribbean Sea. She and Gabriel had sailed all night. He taught her what to do to help him keep the ship on course. The last time they sailed, Ardiel had been with them to help steer the ship while Gabriel manned the sails.

By morning, they were both exhausted. Gabriel set the anchor, and they rested fitfully for as long as they could until the oppressive heat made sleep impossible.

"There look to be islands to the West," Gabriel peered across the water. "Perhaps we can find another village, and start again, more cautiously this time."

For a long moment, Brianna did not answer. The half-Fae man had known exactly where to look for the Sword of Oreveille. Of all the villages in the Caribbean, he had come to theirs.

"Why was he searching for the Sword?" Brianna asked.

"He claimed it belonged to his master, and had been stolen."

"Cordov!" Brianna exclaimed.

Gabriel looked at her, questioning.

"He knew you had the Sword when my mother married him. Without it, his position at Oreveille is not secure. He must have the sword if he is to have any authority at all."

"Let him have it then, and we will have our life here," Gabriel answered.

"He cannot have the Sword. You are the Defender of Oreveille. It is bound to your Spirit, not to his. He cannot so much as touch it."

"How did you touch it then, before your stepfather's death? Was he not the Defender of Oreveille?"

"He was not truly the Defender. The Sword would not bind to him, despite my father's death. It rejected him quite forcefully." Brianna did not bother to hide her smile. "His hand was bruised for weeks."

"It accepted me," Gabriel mused.

"They say the Sword is passed from Defender to Defender. My father must have found you worthy of it."

"So why does Cordov come after it, if he cannot even touch it?"

"He will not need to bind to the Sword himself, or even touch it. As long as he has it at Oreveille, it will be enough. Many families have long since given up the ceremony. The title of Defender is honorary at best. Oreveille is considered quite superstitious that we have performed such ancient rites as recently as my father's time!"

"If he thinks he can take the Sword by main force, or by deceit, all the more reason for us to find a quiet, obscure place to live unnoticed."

"No," Brianna spoke calmly, reminding him once more of the woman he knew in the Faeland. "Obscurity did not hide us, nor did it keep Kathleen and Ardiel safe. Cordov can find the sword, so let him find it. We must focus on keeping it, and ourselves, secure."

"You know I will always protect you," Gabriel swore.

Brianna smiled, and wound her arms around her Defender. "Yes. And I will make certain that Cordov cannot get close enough to harm either of us."

Gabriel laughed, bringing her close. "How do you propose to do that?"

She closed her eyes and relaxed into the warm strength of his body, letting her spirit probe outward until she found what she was looking for.

Brianna turned in his arms and pointed at the rocky cliffs to the west. "There is a cave on that island, and inside, just below the first layer of rock, is a thread of gold six feet thick that winds through the whole mountain. Give me a single day, and I will coax enough gold out of that cave to buy us the richest plantation in the Caribbean. Poverty and hiding did not keep us safe. Wealth, and the power it brings, will."

CHAPTER TWENTY-THREE

May 1649. Isle of Oreveille, Faeland Sea.

Brianna sat on the balcony with Gabriel, sipping wine mixed with fruit. The heat was still oppressive indoors, but the gentle Caribbean breeze made the second-story balcony a pleasant place to sit in the evening. She had insisted that these small balconies be built outside each of the front bedrooms when she commissioned the house. With only two stories, it was smaller than the House on the Isle of Oreveille in the Faeland, but it reminded her of home.

The gardens stretched out before the house almost to the sea, and stone walking paths led throughout the property. If Brianna swept the breeze through the gardens on its way up from the sea, it arrived at the balcony perfumed with bougainvillea.

She spent her days in the first-floor library, which opened into a large conservatory, studying and practicing what she remembered of her lessons in Life magic. This day had been particularly difficult. She had grown bored with her study of plants, but twice she had healed people, and twice had been groping about in the dark, acting on instinct rather than on knowledge. She studied all she could, but without a tutor, she found the boundaries of her abilities all too often.

Gabriel sat next to her, his legs stretched out and relaxed. He spent most of the day in the fields, or with the gardeners, overseeing all the tiny details that went into creating an estate.

"I've hired an overseer," Gabriel mentioned, setting down his wine.

"You should have done so two years ago," Brianna laughed. "Who is he?"

"I wasn't willing to bring on the type of man who calls himself an overseer in these islands. They're small men who live on borrowed power."

Brianna nodded. She had seen the cruelty that passed for discipline on the plantations. In some ways, Gaia and the Faeland were very much alike.

"But I've found a man who can handle the job without letting it go to his head."

"Who?"

"His name's Daniel. He's been working as a laborer on the East garden all summer. I believe he may have Fae blood."

Brianna looked up, her eyes wide with concern. "Get rid of him! He could be one of Cordov's men, sent as a spy."

Gabriel shook his head. "I don't think so. I asked a few questions down in the village. He's grown up here on Martinique. His mother is a seamstress. Gossip has it that one night she rowed out past the harbor and wasn't seen again for a full year. Her people believed she drowned. Then one morning, she rowed back to shore as if nothing ever happened, except she had a newborn baby boy. She's never spoken a word about the father, but the whispers are that her boy has always been a bit strange."

Whispers and rumors. Old stories. Brianna sighed. If this man were half-Fae, perhaps he could be taught to use what Power he might have. If they could gain his trust, he could be a strong ally when Cordov made his next move. Twice in the past five years, Brianna had heard rumors of strangers asking about the Sword of Oreveille, and both times she had been able to deflect suspicion. Cordov was a patient man, but he would not wait forever.

CHAPTER TWENTY-FOUR

Gabriel was glad of the evening breeze. It seemed to blow some of the moisture out of the air, making it almost cool after the heat of the afternoon. The East Garden was finally finished, and he wanted to take Brianna through it. Unlike the formal gardens in the front of the house, this was not designed to impress, but to grow the medicinal herbs she studied. Its beds were laid out to allow for easy reach from all sides, with benches placed throughout for her to sit and read or make sketches. He hoped it would alleviate some of the boredom that had plagued her so often in the last few years.

Leaning on the low stone wall that separated the garden from the lawns, he watched her come down the flagstone pathway from the main house. She walked slowly, as though the heat of the day had dried up the last of her energy. As she neared, he walked down the path to meet her, and to offer his arm.

She rested her arm in his. "They've finished the summer plantings. In a few months, they'll replant and put in the winter plants," Gabriel explained as he led her toward her new garden.

"It will be wonderful. I've been studying how the villagers use preparations made from local plants for healing and for some very simple spirit walking. I want to try to blend that knowledge with what I learned before we left the Faeland," Brianna rambled.

Gabriel nodded. "Be careful. I've heard that some of these plants can be dangerous if they are not prepared properly."

"Every act of healing carries its dangers," Brianna answered. "And it would be foolish not to have a stock of common remedies on hand, in case we need to call the wise woman from the village."

"Why would we need to call her? Are you ill?" Gabriel's concern clouded his voice. Brianna had been so tired recently, and had been spending less and less time in her study.

Brianna shook her head. "No - not ill," She stopped on the path and turned to face him. "But I am tired. And the herbs are for the midwife when she comes."

"The midwife?" Gabriel echoed as he took in her hopeful smile and realized what she meant. "When?"

"In the spring. Plenty of time to prepare," she answered.

Gabriel took in her shining eyes, tight with nerves. The Mark of Oreveille, which she kept so carefully hidden, glowed faintly across her brow. He swept the hair back from her face and smiled, taking his time as he processed this new information. Their baby!

"I love you," he whispered as he kissed her, forgetting all about the garden.

She pulled him closer. "And I, you," she breathed against his lips.

"Master Gabriel!" A breathless voice interrupted their private celebration.

Gabriel lingered for one last moment before turning to see who needed his attention. His new overseer, Daniel, was running hard up the path from the lower orchard.

"What is it?" Gabriel called.

"Is someone hurt?" Brianna added.

"Not yet, Ma'am," Daniel replied, bowing his head to Brianna before he turned to Gabriel. "There's a group of men back in the forest. They're doing their best not to be seen."

"Trappers?" Gabriel asked, doubtfully.

Daniel shook his head. "Unless they plan on trapping within the walls of Oreveille. They're moving this way."

"You know what to do," Gabriel dismissed him.

Daniel nodded once, and set off to gather the men trained to defend the estate.

Gabriel looked at Brianna. "You should wait indoors. The boys and I can take care of this."

"Nonsense," Brianna laughed. "I am not helpless. We will defend Oreveille just as we always do."

Gabriel was unconvinced, but in the end, telling Brianna not to do something was like telling the rain not to fall. He nodded and led the way toward the back wall of the estate.

The men were already in place when Gabriel and Brianna arrived. They stood evenly spaced atop the stone, with crossbows ready. Gabriel had considered purchasing muskets, but Brianna preferred the simplicity of the crossbow, and she was critical to their ability to repel nearly any attack. They would continue to do things her way.

Gabriel closed his eyes, probing outward until he found the group slinking through the trees. A dozen humans, with nothing on their minds but gold and a crude drawing of the Sword of Oreveille.

"Nothing unusual, boys. Just a pack of thieves," he called up to the men on the wall.

They waited, letting the raiders come into view. Gabriel made sure his men kept a fifty-foot swath of land clear between the wall and the forest. If nothing else, it made aiming easier.

At last, the scraggly band of men burst through the trees into the clearing.

Gabriel held up his hand and his men waited. He wanted to be sure the raiders were committed before the archers loosed the arrows. There would not be any survivors left to report back to Cordov.

After several long moments, Gabriel finally glanced back to Brianna. She nodded, and he brought his hand down, signaling the archers to open fire.

The breeze was scarcely noticeable at first. As the arrows arched upward, the wind divided into individual wisps of moving air. Each finger of wind seemed to sweep an arrow out of the sky and hurtle it with perfect aim into the chest of its victim. Not a single one missed its target.

Gabriel watched for a moment, reaching out to each of the motionless figures below. Their minds were blank, their spirits already gone. "All right boys. Go clean up the mess."

He turned back to Brianna. The Mark of Oreveille glowed brightly across her brow, and her eyes shone wild. She may have learned precision, but she still danced on the wind.

CHAPTER TWENTY-FIVE

June, 1655

Brianna focused on the knotted gold rings around her bed. Each was formed to resemble the Mark of Oreveille. None of the servants knew what those knots meant. They only knew that the pattern was repeated throughout the house, and that the Mistress could often be found deep in thought, touching those golden knots.

Today, Brianna simply stared up at them as she clutched the damp cotton sheets with each contraction. Her moans seemed to come from somewhere far away. Gabriel sat next to the bed, touching her hand, comforting her as best he could from outside the tiny circle of her immediate awareness.

Somewhere in the room, Marie, the Caribbean midwife, moved about. She had been West African once, a lifetime ago, but her many decades among the islands had altered her to the core. She spoke, but Brianna could not understand her. Kathleen seemed to be next to her, guiding and directing everyone in the room. Brianna could not turn her head to see, and Gabriel did not speak to his mother, who had gone into the mists so many years ago, but Brianna smiled, knowing she was there. Kathleen would bring her granddaughter safely into the world.

"Push now, Ma'am," The midwife's voice was gentle and commanding. "This baby's gonna come just fine now."

"Is it time?" Gabriel asked. He had broken tradition and taboo by insisting upon staying in the birthing room, and the midwife had only allowed it because "the old lady said it would be all right." No one had questioned her, and Gabriel had not moved from his seat next to the bed in several hours.

Brianna pushed, gently at first. She tried to use what she had learned of healing to check the infant's health, but the pain and confusion were too great. She could not send her spirit out, even into her own body. It refused to obey.

"Come on now, let's birth this baby now," Marie repeated, her voice mesmerizing.

Brianna pushed again and again, harder each time. Finally, the head and shoulders slipped out and Brianna collapsed back onto the pillows, exhausted.

Moments later, Marie placed the infant, wrapped in a warmed sheet, into Brianna's arms. She looked at her daughter, this impossible new creature.

"Welcome, Daughter of Oreveille," Brianna whispered as she traced the Mark on the infant's forehead. As her fingers moved, the design appeared: a sword woven into knotted gold.

Brianna smiled as her eyes met Gabriel's.

"She will be strong," Brianna murmured. "Look how brightly the Mark glows."

Gabriel kissed his daughter's forehead. "She will be like her mother."

Without a word, Marie slipped from the room.

Tricia Ballad

CHAPTER TWENTY-SIX

Over the next several days, Brianna settled into a routine. As the sun rose, Marie brought the infant, named Kathleen in honor of her grandmother, to nurse. Once mother and baby were settled, she opened the French doors to let in the morning breeze before hurrying downstairs to assist the cook with the day's baking.

Today, however, she lingered.

"Is something wrong, Marie?"

"No Ma'am," she assured Brianna. "I just wondered… the birthmark on the baby's forehead…"

Brianna smiled as she looked down at her infant daughter. Whenever she fed the baby girl, the Mark of Oreveille glowed brighter.

"It will not harm her," Brianna dismissed the other woman.

"No Ma'am," Marie continued. "But…I heard stories of powerful Voudou Queens who had marks like that. Priest says it's the mark of the Devil."

Brianna looked at the woman's impossibly black eyes, set deep and hidden in her dark face. She saw fear in those eyes, but something else as well. Something behind the fear.

"What devil?" Brianna could not keep the derision out of her voice. The Priest was not the most insightful of men. He saw devils everywhere he looked. "There is no devil here. You may rest easy, Marie. There is Power, and that is all."

Brianna looked up from the drowsing infant at her breast. Marie still hesitated, waiting.

"What is it?" Brianna asked the midwife and nursemaid. "Does it frighten you?"

Marie shook her head. "No Ma'am. My mother and grandmother spoke with the spirits, back at home. I was starting to learn when I was brought here when I was just a girl." She stopped, as though afraid to reveal more.

"And you wish to learn?" Brianna finished for her.

Marie's face remained neutral as she searched her Mistress for any sign of deception or trickery. Brianna waited. Finally, Marie nodded. "Yes Ma'am. To protect the baby from whatever may come."

Brianna smiled. "Yes. She must be protected from my enemies, who would use her to attack me."

Marie nodded. "Yes Ma'am."

"The world passes through cycles of high and low energy. The cycles begin and end with the lives of the King and Queen."

Brianna paused in her explanation. "Do you know of this?"

Marie shook her head. "No Ma'am. In our village, we spoke of the old ones, spirits older than the earth itself. We do not know of your kings and queens."

"They govern the cycles. One of the Fae and one of Gaia must come together. When they meet, the cycle is born, and it dies when they die."

Marie stared at her mistress. "Are you...?"

Brianna laughed. "The queen of this cycle? Hardly. I do not even know her. My House guards the very border of the Faeland. We did not travel to other regions," she smiled, remembering the Isle of Oreveille.

Marie stared harder. "The Fae land?"

Brianna looked at the other woman, and realized she had perhaps been too candid. Even here, rumors of witchcraft were not easily dismissed.

"We can continue this another time. Kathleen is finished eating, and I would like a warm bath before I come downstairs," Brianna ordered.

"Yes Ma'am. I will send the maids up," Marie replied, taking the infant.

Brianna watched her go, and sighed, remembering Oreveille. She wondered if her mother sensed Kathleen's birth, or if the House of Oreveille still stood. She closed her eyes against vivid imaginings of Oreveille destroyed, its people scattered. Surely, if her House had fallen, she would know.

CHAPTER TWENTY-SEVEN

Brianna rocked in the twilight, letting the quiet evening breeze calm her nerves.

"Shall I take the baby, Ma'am?" Marie spoke softly, unwilling disturb the sleeping infant.

"No, I'll bring her in later," Brianna smiled at her daughter, nestled safely in her arms. Marie nodded and faded back into the house.

Gabriel sat nearby, looking out over the estate that never seemed to be finished. He was describing the new bunkhouse he planned to build. In the last year, he had brought home several more half-Fae. Some had been mere children living on scraps in the villages of Martinique. Others used their meager power to improve their standing in Gaian society, and came to Gabriel and

Brianna to learn more. Most, however, were half-mad drunkards who used rum to drown out the voices of spirits and to soothe their fear of devils. To these, Gabriel simply offered a haven. He gave them honest work, good food, and assurances that there were far more saints than devils. He did what he could for them.

Brianna blinked, startled from her daydreams by a change in the air and the sound of footsteps on the stone pathway toward the house. Before she could speak, Gabriel was already on his feet, ready to greet the newcomer.

"Marie," Brianna summoned the nurse, who was never far from the baby. "Take Kathleen inside."

Marie nodded, cuddling infant close.

The man paused at the base of the steps. His silvery blond hair shone in the moonlight, despite streaks of grey. He was thinner than she remembered him. The faint glow of the Mark of Oreveille shone just above his eyes.

"Cordov…" her composure faltered as she recognized the man she had fought at a distance for so long. She took a breath, unwilling to allow his presence to shake her. "Cordov of Oreveille."

The man nodded. "Your mother sends her greetings. May I enter?" His voice was calm.

"Of course," Brianna stepped closer to Gabriel to give Cordov room to pass. "You should at least have taken care to appear human before coming here," she spoke under her breath as he walked past her.

Cordov nodded. "Perhaps. You need not worry, your servants will not recall my visit."

Brianna relaxed a bit. Cordov had studied influence, and by now would be able to easily manipulate the memories or impressions of a handful of humans and half-Fae who may have noticed him - if it suited his purposes, of course.

She led the way into the front parlor and chose a large cushioned chair flanked by long windows. As she walked into the room, the candles began to glow. Gabriel stood beside her, with the Sword of Oreveille hung above them. It was not quite a throne room, but the ornate woodwork and arrangement of the room was designed to intimidate. Brianna gestured to the seats clustered around her. "Would you care for some refreshment?"

Cordov shook his head and remained standing. "Perhaps another time, D'Oreveille. My business with you is quite pressing, and I cannot stay long on Gaia."

"What message do you bring? Is my mother…?" She left the words hanging. The Council may have disowned her, but Brianna was still the only heir to Oreveille. If her mother were dying, they may send for her to return and take her place rather than dissolve the ancient estate.

"Your mother is in excellent heath," Cordov reported. "I do not come at the bidding of the Council or anyone else. Perhaps you are aware that the cycle is waning?"

Brianna thought for a moment. It had been getting more difficult, taking more energy and concentration recently, to do even simple tasks. If the magical cycle were waning, that would explain it. She nodded for him to continue.

"I have identified the king and queen of the next cycle. You realize that if they meet, Gaia will enter a time without magic."

Brianna nodded impatiently. "I understand the cycles, Cordov."

"And where does that leave you and your little play house?" He sneered, glancing at the candles and the wooden fan hung from the ceiling. When Brianna entered the room it had begun to sway, creating a gentle breeze.

She sighed. As hard as she tried, old habits were hard to break. "You came here, and put me and my family at risk, simply to warn me that I'll have to tell a servant to light the candles and start the fans moving?" she demanded.

"You always were a stupid girl!" Cordov stepped toward her.

"You're going to want to sit down." Gabriel's voice was hard in the soft candlelight. The Sword of Oreveille pulsed at his words.

Cordov eyed Gabriel, and stepped back from Brianna. "Perhaps I was foolish to think I needed the help of a Fae woman. Perhaps it's a human man that I need," he smiled. "How much do you know of the cycles?" he asked Gabriel.

"I know enough. What do you want?" Gabriel asked.

"The queen is in a village not far from here. She will meet her king very soon – perhaps even within the next month. When they meet, the cycle will shift, and with their union, all magic will cease on Gaia for a generation or more. No one knows how long the cycle will last," Cordov spoke quickly.

"Fine. What does this have to do with us?" Gabriel demanded. "We can live without magic here. Go back to the Faeland where you belong."

Cordov smiled. "No magic at all?" he pressed, looking at Brianna.

Gabriel followed his glance. "Bri?"

She folded her hands in her lap and looked at her husband. "Just glamour, to appear human," she hesitated, wondering if she could trust Cordov to keep her secret. She shook her head. If she had to choose one man in the room to trust, she would choose Gabriel and disarm Cordov in the process. "And some healing. I have never been able to fully heal your old wound. I do not know how. But I know enough to keep the shard from cutting into your heart, and to prevent infection. It is nothing anyone would ever notice unless they knew what to look for."

"When the magic flees Gaia, she will not have the power to keep that splinter of steel from piercing your heart, dealing the death blow that should have been yours so many years ago," Cordov smiled. "Infection will set in, you will weaken, and your last days, I would imagine, would not be pleasant ones."

Brianna gripped her husband's hand as she listened to their fate. "Surely you did not come here just to frighten us with tales of unavoidable death. What do you want?" she demanded.

"Kill the queen," Cordov said simply. "Kill her, and the cycles do not change. We remain in a time of magic, and you go on living your simple little lives. Do this one small task, and I will not even mention your unorthodox healing methods in the village tavern. You know the Priest is burning with curiosity…"

CHAPTER TWENTY-EIGHT

Gabriel stared at Cordov. "You expect us to kill an innocent girl?"

Cordov shrugged. "Sometimes an innocent must die to save the world. It is the way of things."

Brianna held her head high. "And what do you gain from her death?"

"Brianna!" Gabriel said her name in shock. "You can't be serious."

"I would survive the change. You would not. Cordov was telling me that what I would have to stand by, helplessly, and watch," Brianna's eyes were wet with tears. "We will make the girl's death quick and painless. I will give her a sleeping draught, and she will slide into a beautiful dream and follow it peacefully into the mists."

Gabriel let go of Brianna's hands. "No. We will not do this. We've left our home before; we can do it again. Perhaps we can get back to the Faeland before the cycle changes."

Cordov nodded in agreement. "You could, certainly. I would be happy to escort you myself. The Council of Matriarchs has offered a generous reward to anyone who delivers the man who kidnapped the lovely Brianna D'Oreveille, and I would be most interested in seeing you hang for your crimes. The Sword of Oreveille will be mine," His voice lost its smooth edge as he glanced over Gabriel's shoulder at the Sword.

Brianna stood beside Gabriel, silently watching as he struggled with the reality of the situation. "What do you have to gain from the girl's death?"

Cordov opened his hands, regaining control. "My interests, at the moment, are the same as yours, D'Oreveille. With the queen dead, the cycles remain unchanged, and the passages between Gaia and the Faeland remain open for another generation. My business continues to grow, and my power with it," he glanced around the opulent room. "You well know how easy it is to exchange gold for power."

"Commit your own crimes, Cordov," Gabriel growled. "I will not kill for you again."

Cordov smiled. "I will leave you to discuss. You will find Catherine Miller in the village of Ansolm. In or near the church, unless I miss my guess." He bowed to Brianna, who nodded out of long ingrained habit.

Brianna did not notice as Cordov left the house. Her attention was on Gabriel. Cordov had laid out their options with brutal honesty. They could not remain once magic left Gaia or Gabriel would die. They could not flee back to the Faeland, or his life was forfeit.

"We have no choice, can you not see that?" Desperation made Brianna's voice shrill.

"What about the dark age?" Gabriel reminded her.

"What dark age?" Brianna asked. "Life is good, and I do not need much power to sustain you. There is no dark age coming."

"Da told me once, if the cycles do not turn when they're meant to, a dark age descends. Wars, famine, drought, and disease all converge," Gabriel explained.

"I doubt that one couple meeting – or not – is enough to throw the world into war and famine and disease," Brianna pointed out.

"Those are the legends," Gabriel insisted.

"They are just legends," Brianna countered. "In the morning, I am going to Ansolm to find this Catherine Miller." She stood taller, reminding Gabriel - and herself - that she was, in fact, a woman of the Fae and accustomed to doing as she wished.

"Do not harm the girl," Gabriel commanded.

Brianna raised her eyebrows in surprise. Even in Gaia, Gabriel did not often presume to tell her what to do.

"I will do what I must!" She countered.

CHAPTER TWENTY-NINE

Early the next morning, Brianna slipped out of Gabriel's sleeping embrace. She shivered against the cold, and against the thing she must do. They had argued long into the night, and in the end neither had been willing to give ground. Brianna did what she had to do – she lied, and told him she would not harm the girl. Perhaps she could convince him that if the girl felt no pain, then no harm was done. Brianna shrugged as she soundlessly put on a simple gown and let herself out of the house. It was a long walk to Ansolm, and she had to be far enough ahead to do the deed before Gabriel caught up to her.

It was fully morning by the time Brianna saw the steeple of the church at the center of Ansolm. As Cordov had predicted, a young woman sat on the steps, toying with the silver crucifix at her throat. She shifted, looking first toward the small rectory, then in the opposite direction toward the outskirts of town. Brianna watched her for several minutes as she waited. The girl could not be more than fifteen years old. She was too young to carry the weight of two worlds in her heart.

Brianna studied the girl and worked out what to say to her. When she left the estate earlier in the morning, it all seemed so simple – find the girl, give her the sleeping potion, and get home. She would face Gabriel's wrath, but at least he would be alive. Now, seeing her sit on the steps of the church, Brianna realized she had no idea what to say to the young girl. "Drink this" did not sound particularly convincing. As Brianna considered several possible stories, the girl stood up to greet the aging priest who walked up the church steps.

"Good morning, Father," the girl said.

"Good morning Catherine," the Priest replied. "And what heinous crime have you managed to commit since yesterday?"

Catherine lowered her eyes and spoke too softly for Brianna to hear. The priest took her hands. "My girl, we have been over this. Dreams are outside of your control, and are not sins."

The girl looked up. Brianna could see the imploring look she gave the old man. She seemed downright terrified of whatever she had dreamed. "Please, Father! I need absolution, so that I can face this day with a clean heart," the girl repeated her request. "Perhaps if I can remain pure all day, the dreams will not touch me again this night."

Brianna smiled. Was that all? Catherine was very young, and was dreaming of her king. Of course she had no idea what to make of it all. She watched as the Priest dutifully led the young girl into the church. Fifteen minutes later, the girl emerged, looking radiant and at peace. It was time for Brianna to make her move. Let the girl move into the mists in such a state of peace. She approached the church and waited for the girl.

"Catherine," Brianna called.

The young girl turned around, startled. "Yes?"

"If you have a moment, I would speak with you about your dreams," Brianna got straight to the point. The day was getting warm, and by now Gabriel would have woken to find her gone.

The girl shook her head. "Those dreams will not trouble me again. My soul is clean." She smiled, although Brianna sensed that she was not nearly as certain of that as she claimed.

"You have been dreaming of a man, have you not? The same man comes to you every night, and has been for some time," Brianna pressed her advantage.

The girl did not answer, but she did not deny it either.

"He will be here in the flesh soon. The dreams are simply to prepare you for what is to come," Brianna told her.

"No! I cannot! Surely I could not…" the girl blushed a deep scarlet.

"And more," Brianna smiled wickedly.

Catherine shook her head. "No! Who are you, that you know of my dreams?"

"I am a wise woman, and have seen young girls in your plight many times before. It happens this way sometimes," Brianna lowered her voice dramatically. She wasn't quite sure where she was going with this story, but she would follow it through. "A man of magic, strong magic at that, finds a sweetly innocent, beautiful young girl. Instead of meeting her like an honest man, and appealing to her father for permission to court her, he comes to her where she is most vulnerable, in her dreams. Eventually, he knows that the pleasures he brings will be too much for her to resist, and she will fall into his arms any time he chooses. He will be gone soon after, of course, but by then she is his creature, and will give him whatever he wants for the rest of her life," Brianna wove the dark story, making sure to hit all the elements that would frighten a young girl overly interested in purity.

Catherine's eyes grew wide as she listened to Brianna's story. She clasped the sleeve of the older woman's gown. "Please, you must help me! How might I escape from this man, when I do not know his face?"

"You do not see his face in your dreams?" Brianna asked.

Catherine shook her head. "No. He is always wearing a cloak that hides his face. Surely no honest man would hide thus!"

Brianna put an arm around the young girl and reached into her pouch. She felt the cold glass vial she had prepared long after Gabriel had fallen asleep. His face floated in her mind, and she remembered his voice. "Put her in a convent or something. There are ways to prevent them from meeting – you do not have to kill her. You are not a murderer!" Brianna softly dropped the vial. He was right. This girl did not even want to meet her king. If anything, she was begging Brianna to protect her from meeting him. It would be easy enough.

"Why have you not entered a convent?" Brianna broached the subject. "I can see that you are a devout girl, with great faith in God," she added.

"My father will not allow it," Catherine replied desperately. "I have begged, but he insists that I must marry. I am only allowed to come to the church every three days, but sometimes I sneak out before dawn for absolution," the girl confessed.

Brianna nodded in pretended understanding. "There is a cloister half a day's journey from here. Once you go and say your vows, your father cannot force you to leave," She mentioned. "I am sure the sisters would arrange for a Priest to hear your confession after you have taken your novitiate. Many of them had no choice but to seek their vows secretly."

Catherine's eyes lit up in hope. "Truly? I did not know there was a community so close by! Could you… perhaps…?" The girl left her request unspoken.

Brianna smiled. "I would be happy to escort you to the convent, my girl. Surely once you are within those sacred walls your dreams will trouble you no more."

Catherine smiled. "Surely they will not. Let us be off, and quickly, before my father notices that I have not yet fed the pigs."

Brianna nodded, and led the young girl out of the village.

CHAPTER THIRTY

They walked half a day to the North until they reached the craggy coastline. There they turned West, and followed the shore until they came upon the Cloister of Saint Agnes. Brianna nodded to Catherine, who slowly tapped the great knocker on the massive oak door.

As they waited for admittance, another group of travelers came around the stone wall that defended the cloister. Brianna's stomach clenched. Two men leaning on each other for support in their wounds, made their way toward the sisters' door. "Two boys..." Brianna amended her initial assessment. Neither of them looked old enough to call them men. Eighteen, perhaps. She briefly wondered what skirmish left them so far away from home, with so much blood on their cloaks.

Catherine knocked again, intent upon gaining admittance to the cloister.

"Please, answer the door!" Brianna prayed silently, wishing she had any skill whatsoever at spirit walking or influence. "Perhaps there is another door," she suggested to Catherine, as the two men drew nearer. "If the sisters are in the garden, they may not hear the door."

Catherine nodded. "Perhaps you are right." She looked up and noticed their companions for the first time. The two men approached the door.

"Good morning, ladies." The taller man swept off his hat in as much of a bow as he could manage without dropping his bleeding friend.

Catherine dropped instantly into a pretty curtsy. "Good morning, sir." As she stood, she looked into the eyes of her king, and Brianna felt a wave of pure energy pass through her as it rushed out from the young couple. The air chilled around her, as the magical energy in the air evaporated. She gasped, as she realized how quickly power began to flee. She thought it would take days or weeks, not just a few moments!

"I must go," Brianna said to Catherine. "Get into the cloister, take your vows," she commanded. "I will come visit you in a few weeks' time, after you've taken your vows!" she repeated.

Catherine looked confused, but waved as her guide and companion fled back toward the village.

Once she was out of sight, Brianna stopped. She held her moonstone tightly within her fist and communed with Air, rising off the ground to float. She had to reach

Gabriel, and fast, before the wave of power left him dead or dying. Already she could feel herself growing tired, but she could not stop to worry about that. Once they reached the Faeland, she would have time to rest.

Brianna flew over the forests, just above the trees, and prayed no one saw her. She had no time to be subtle. If the Priest or one of the villagers saw her soaring through the sky, it would confirm even the wildest rumors that she dabbled in witchcraft. But none of that would matter for much longer. If her luck held, she and Gabriel would dine at the House of Oreveille this evening.

She carefully lowered herself to the ground in the rose garden Gabriel had built for her last year. It was one of her favorite places on the estate, and she would miss it. Perhaps…Brianna smiled. Perhaps she would leave the estate to Marie. It would give her, and the half-Fae Gabriel had gathered together, a safe place to live and practice their gifts. Brianna nodded. She would rather see her home in the hands of those she trusted than fought over and carved up by the local plantation owners. Marie was a capable woman, with a good mind and enough power to carry out her will. She would care for the estate and its people.

Tricia Ballad

CHAPTER THIRTY-ONE

Gabriel rolled over in his sleep and gasped at the sharp pain near his heart. Opening his eyes, he sat up to get a deeper breath. The room was too silent. Brianna was gone. He took another breath. They had gone to bed the night before, angry and silent, without reaching common ground. They had simply collapsed, having run out of things to say.

He stood up from the empty bed. He should have known she would do what she wanted to do. She pretended to listen to his concerns, but in the end, she had already made up her mind. Like every Fae noblewoman, she did not allow a man - much less one of human blood - to get in her way.

He walked through the quiet house, half hoping to find Brianna sleeping in a chair in one of the parlors. Instead he found Cordov sitting in the front parlor with the Sword of Oreveille hanging above his head. The Fae man lounged in the cushioned chair, idly flipping through one of the many books in the room.

Cordov glanced up when Gabriel entered the room. "You played your part well, you know," Cordov congratulated him. "She would have resisted my influence much more effectively had you not played the moralist."

"Brianna does what she wants to do. She always has."

Cordov laughed. "Yes, that's what we let them think, isn't it? Fae woman are much more compliant when they think they are getting their own way. Spoiled brats, every one of them," he spat out. "It's why I like a nice, simple human wench. They do what they're told to do without all the tiresome arguing."

Gabriel lunged, ready to hurl Cordov out of the chair.

Cordov laughed. His face shifted, growing larger and more elemental. All semblance of sophistication faded from his eyes as his cheekbones grew more prominent and his skin more leathery.

It was too late for Gabriel to stop before he rushed into the waiting arms of the jotnar, who only a moment before had been a perfect illusion of Cordov.

Gabriel ducked as the beast wrapped its claws around the space his head should have been, and slammed his shoulder into the creature's side. He gasped as the stabbing pain near his heart brought him to his knees.

The jotnar's roar shook the windows, breaking the nighttime stillness. It hovered over Gabriel, its jaws dripping in anticipation, but it did not devour him. Instead, it looked to its master. Gabriel fought to keep conscious, as the pain in his heart grew stronger with every movement.

Cordov stepped out of the shadows. "Perhaps I should let the beast have its supper," he mused. "It hasn't eaten in weeks. Perhaps...but first you have some work to do, Defender of Oreveille," he sneered, grabbing Gabriel by the hair.

The jotnar moaned, salivating. It reached for Gabriel, then pulled its claw back to its mouth, never taking its eyes off Cordov.

"Give me the Sword of Oreveille," Cordov commanded.

Gabriel blinked. Somehow, Cordov had concealed a jotnar on Gaia. Magic had not faded. Brianna had stopped the cycles.

"The Sword!" The fear in Cordov's voice betrayed him.

"Take it yourself," Gabriel spoke. "Once I'm dead, take the Sword and Brianna back to the Faeland. She's made her choice."

"I have made my choice," Brianna's voice came through the darkness. "Catherine lives, and she has met her king."

The jotnar's eyes grew wide as it realized that Cordov's bond of influence had disappeared. It forgot about Gabriel, and advanced on the Fae man who had kept it bound and starving for so many weeks.

Cordov heard Brianna's declaration and fled the house with the jotnar roaring in pursuit.

CHAPTER THIRTY-TWO

Brianna reached out with her spirit to see how badly Gabriel was injured, but she could not feel the familiar pathways of his heart and lungs. Her vision stopped at his skin, as though she had no more power than a human child.

She helped him stand, and held him as he struggled for breath.

"Gabriel. We must get to the Faeland. There are healers at Oreveille."

Gabriel lifted his head. "You did not kill her?"

Brianna shook her head. "No. I took her to a convent, but it was too late. I took her to the place where she met her king!" She sucked in a deep breath. "I failed."

"Why would a Fae healer save the life of a human?" Gabriel struggled to stand.

"Because I command it," Brianna spoke with the full force of a Fae noblewoman. She gripped his body and moved as fast as she could with his extra weight. All of her concentration and energy was invested in reaching the border of the Faeland before the portal closed and she was trapped as a widow in the human lands. Gabriel did not fight her.

She half-carried him out of the house. "Please, we must get to Oreveille, before we are trapped here!" She could not carry him all the way to the dock. It was too far.

"Marie!" Brianna screamed into the house.

The nursemaid appeared from the kitchens. "Lady? What's happened?"

"I cannot stop to explain. We must go to the Faeland to save Master Gabriel's life. The estate is yours. Take care of Kathleen. I will return for her as soon as I can. Please, help me to the dock!" Brianna begged.

Marie helped her carry Gabriel to the dock. The two women made him as comfortable as they could.

"I will care for the child like she was my own flesh and blood," Marie promised.

"I know you will. You love her nearly as much as I do," Brianna smiled. "Care for the plantation and its people, and they will be loyal to you. I will return as soon as I can."

"Good luck, Madame," Marie shoved the small boat away from the dock, and Brianna used the last of her power to call the Air to puff out the sails. She worked furiously to guide the small boat to where she thought the border between the Caribbean Sea and the Faeland might be.

Brianna stood near the sails, as Gabriel instructed her in the tasks she must perform to sail the boat toward the borderlands. For hours, it seemed as though they did nothing but sail in circles, as Gabriel grew weaker and weaker.

Brianna relaxed slightly when she passed over the invisible barrier between the two worlds, and felt the warm glow of magical energy. She did not realize how comforting it was until it was gone. She looked around and remembered the last time she sailed this sea. She and Gabriel had been fleeing for their lives then too.

She sent her spirit into Gabriel. The sliver of steel was lodged firmly within his heart. It was too deep to dare moving it, so she simply did what she could to lessen the pain until they arrived at Oreveille.

Soon the villa appeared on the horizon. Her mother may not like her arriving thus, but she would accept her. She must accept her own daughter. Brianna began to doubt for the first time. If her mother truly disowned her, she was not sure what she would do next. She shook her head. All she could do was hope for the best.

Gabriel was limp in her arms by the time she landed at the dock. She took to the Air, floating to the garden outside the front door of the villa. The door opened, and Madame D'Oreveille stood in the foyer, awaiting explanation from her daughter who had reappeared so suddenly.

"Mother. Please. Call a healer. Gabriel is dying. I need your help," Brianna choked out the words, fearing that it was already too late.

Madame D'Oreveille nodded, seeing the situation for what it was. "Take him to the rose chamber," she ordered, as a servant stepped silently forward to relieve Brianna of her burden.

Brianna smiled at her mother's peace offering. The rose chamber had been hers all those decades ago. "Thank you," she said, following the servant up the stairs.

The healer arrived soon after, and did what he could, but even he could not repair Gabriel's shredded heart. Brianna held Gabriel's hand as he fought to stay with her on this side of the mists.

"Bri," Gabriel whispered.

"I am here, my love," she answered.

"I am not leaving you. I will return," he muttered.

Brianna nodded to the dying man.

"We do not part at death. That was not part of the vow," he spoke more clearly, though it cost him his last drop of energy.

"Gabriel…" Brianna whispered as he closed his eyes for the last time. She looked to the healer, who shook his head. Her mother sat next to her and held her as she wept for the man she was not able to save.

FROM BOOK TWO: DEFENDER OF OREVEILLE

1702, Isle of Oreveille, Faeland Sea

Brianna sat on the balcony the next morning, enjoying the early summer breeze as she drank her tea. She should have been relaxed. The Solstice ball was over for another year, and she had no commitments until later that evening. Yet she could not seem to sit still. Something was off. She thought back over the last few days. Nothing extraordinary had happened, or was going to happen. Things were relatively calm, for once. Brianna set down her teacup and called for her maid. Perhaps a walk around the estate would clear her mind.

She dressed simply, in a light green gown that would not catch and rip on the brambles if she should decide to leave the walkways. As she walked through the house,

Brianna was relieved that the servants faded out of her path, disappearing into doorways and side rooms.

Fresh air was exactly what she needed, Brianna decided, as she wandered out of the rose garden toward the orchard. She would check the trees, to see if she could expect a good harvest this year. Strident male voices broke her peaceful silence. She stopped at the top of a hill to see what was happening below. She saw the gardener, an old half-Fae with a vicious temper, waving his fist at a man climbing up one of the trees. Her breath caught in her lungs as the memories came flooding back. But this was not her Gabriel, she reminded herself. This was the new human slave the men had captured yesterday. Still, the resemblance was unsettling.

"I will return." Brianna could still hear Gabriel's dying words, so many decades later. She shook her head. She did not have time for fantasies. Striding down the hill, she summoned the gardener.

"Get that human out of my orchard!" Brianna's voice rose petulantly.

Darien, the gardener, did not meet her eyes. None of the servants did. "Aye, Madam. You'd like him at the house?" he asked.

Brianna went cold. This human, who made her think of Gabriel, in the house? "No. I do not use humans in the house. Put him in the stables, or the grain fields, or anywhere else. But I do not want this one in the orchards!" Brianna repeated.

"Aye, Madam." Darien bowed as Brianna hurried out of the orchards without looking at the man whose presence so disturbed her.

*****

Gabe climbed out of the cherry tree, grinning. He had no idea why the mistress of the house was so upset, but it appeared that Fae women were not so different from human ones. He had grown up listening to his mother and sisters carry on in exactly the same tone over similarly meaningless crises.

"Get ye to the stables, human." Darien ordered, pointing the way.

Gabe ducked and started walking the direction the gardener indicated. He didn't mind horses. They were a sight more rational than women, most of the time.

As he entered the darkness of the barn, the horses began pawing their stalls and whinnying. He walked up to one of them and spoke softly, and the horse quieted. One by one, he quieted the horses that were so disturbed by his entrance.

Looking around, he noticed that the stalls had not been cleaned out in some time. The straw was rancid and matted with filth.

"When was the last time you were out of this barn, girl?" he asked one particularly shy mare. The horse nuzzled him in answer. He patted her mane. "I'll be right back." He promised softly, soothing the nervous horse, as he went in search of a bridle.

"There is nothing worth stealing, and these horses will not carry you off my lands." Gabe heard a cold woman's voice behind him. He turned and saw the mistress of the house standing, silhouetted in the doorway of the barn.

"I'd be surprised if these horses could carry themselves, let alone a full-grown man." Gabe answered her. "For a woman who's particular about who trims her cherry trees, you don't take much notice of the horses, do you?"

Brianna stared at this human who dared scold her about the state of her stables. "You dare speak to me so?" she asked, her voice barely above a whisper.

"Apparently I do." Gabe grinned. "Now, if you'll kindly get out of my way, there's a barn full of horses in great need of some fresh air and new straw. Nobody else around here seems likely to take care of it."

"I ought to have you flogged." Brianna said.

"For taking care of your neglected horses? Nay – flog the man who should have been mucking out these stalls. I'll do the floggin' myself, as soon as the horses are bedded down." Gabe answered, shouldering past Brianna with a filthy leather bridle.

Speechless, Brianna watched him lead the mare out into the practice yard, then return with a shovel to clean out the stall. One by one, he led each of the horses out into the yard, and did not say another word to her. As long as she did not interfere with him, she could stand there in the barn and watch honest work all day if it suited her. Judging from the look of her, it may be the first time she'd ever seen anything like it.

It was late in the day by the time the stable was fit for horses again. He examined each of them quickly, and was relieved that he saw no signs of illness or injury. He would do a more thorough examination in the morning, he decided, as he walked back to the cottage he had shared with the under gardener, Bard, last night.

He went inside and sat down. Bard was not there, which gave Gabe time to think. This little house reminded him of something that he could not quite grasp. Everywhere he looked, he seemed to remember moments, people – but they were another man's memories, not his own. He remembered a raven-haired girl in a deep green dress laughing, pulling him toward the door. But not him. The man in his memories did not look like Gabe, he looked like the half-Fae gardeners and servants that swarmed the estate. Gabe shook his head. He didn't know what magic was going on. All he knew was that for the first time in his life, he felt strangely at home.

*****

I hope you enjoyed Daughter of Oreveille. Stop by www.TriciaBallad.com to find out more about the Faeland and the stories it contains.

-- Tricia Ballad

Tricia Ballad

ABOUT THE AUTHOR

Tricia Ballad started making up stories as soon as she was old enough to talk, and began writing them down soon after.

When she could not find a story to fit her mood, she wrote one. And in one way or another, she's been writing ever since.

After spending most of her childhood cavorting with words when she should have been learning algebra, she came up for air in college, did her fair share of stupid things, met the love of her life, and managed to graduate with a degree in creative writing.

Tricia spent the next decade in a haze of sleep deprivation and diapers. When she finally remembered how to sleep again, she returned to writing stories. Her debut novel, Daughter of Oreveille, was released in August 2013.

Tricia lives in Illinois with her husband, four children, and assorted other creatures. She is fairly certain there is a family of coffee-stealing gnomes hiding in the walls.